The Swiss finishing school found her too hot to handle...

Her society mother wanted to lock her up behind prison bars . . .

The private eye who'd been hired to tail her turned up with his skull bashed in . . .

Her name was Angela Summers and she was anything but an angel. Everywhere she went, she courted trouble. But this time it was different. Murder was too way out for kicks, so she asked Al Wheeler, the free-wheeling cop, to help prove her innocence.

In this hot and heady thriller by the international sensation whose mysteries have sold almost twenty-eight million copies, **AL WHEELER** tangles with a teen-age temptress and her beatnik boy friend, a sex-mad millionaire, a luscious lady lawyer, and the corpse of a private eye who stuck his head out —once too often.

carter brown

The Temptress

 A SIGNET BOOK
Published by
THE NEW AMERICAN LIBRARY OF WORLD LITERATURE,
INC.
in association with
HORWITZ PUBLICATIONS, INC.

SIGNET TRADEMARK REG. U.S. PAT. OFF. AND FOREIGN COUNTRIES
REGISTERED TRADEMARK—MARCA REGISTRADA
HECHO EN CHICAGO, U.S.A.

SIGNET BOOKS are published by
The New American Library, Inc.
1301 Avenue of the Americas, New York, New York 10019

PRINTED IN THE UNITED STATES OF AMERICA

· 1 ·

HE LAY FACE DOWN ON A SAGGING BED IN ONE OF THE cabins belonging to a cheap motel which the proprietor with a sardonic sense of humor had called The Travelers' Rest. A shaft of sunlight through the dust-hazed window lit one side of his face and he didn't even look surprised.

Maybe there are some nice ways to die but having the back of your skull beaten into a gray-flecked, blood-soaked pulp isn't one of them.

I lit a cigarette, waiting until Doc Murphy straightened his back with a faint grunt of relief and looked at me, his face a couple of shades paler than usual.

"The proverbial blunt instrument as we already know, Wheeler," he said gruffly. "Did quite a job on him, whoever it was, didn't they?"

It was a question without need of an answer. I followed him into the bathroom and watched him run the cold tap, washing his hands with professional thoroughness.

"Any one of the blows, administered with the force they were, would have killed him," he said bleakly.

"Including the first one?"

"Exactly right, Lieutenant," he nodded. "He was hit a dozen times, maybe more." He shuddered slightly as he looked at the dirty gray towel on the rack beside the washbasin, then used his pocket handkerchief to dry his hands.

"You're looking for a maniac, Wheeler!"

"Yeah," I said absently. "You all through, Doc?"

"Sure—he's all yours!"

It was my turn to grimace as I walked back into the other room. The two crime lab boys I'd borrowed from Homicide had finished up and were already on their way back to town, taking the rusty hammer along with them, wrapped carefully in a nice clean cloth. The hammer had been on the floor alongside the bed, its business end encrusted with a mixture of hair and dried blood.

The shaft of sunlight still lit the side of his face, and when I turned the body over gently onto its back, the whole face had the same look of not being even surprised. The wide-open eyes looked at me with a calm, even remote, expression.

A guy in his early forties, with thinning brown hair and a sharp pointed nose—a small, lightweight guy who wouldn't have gone heavier than 140 on the scales, stripped. He was fully dressed in a crumpled tan wash-and-wear suit; with a cheap white no-iron shirt and clumsily knotted necktie underneath. On his feet were dirty, scuffed, brown suede shoes. He didn't look like he'd been a success.

I went through his pockets systematically and came up with a handkerchief, car keys, a handful of small change, and a billfold. I emptied the contents of the billfold out onto the cigarette-burned top of the dressing table. A hundred dollars in fives and tens, a New York State private detective's license made out to Albert H. Marvin, a driver's license, and a couple of receipted bills—one from a motel in Santa Monica, dated three days before, and one from this motel.

Doc Murphy made a rasping sound in his throat as he peered over my shoulder.

"Private eye, huh?" he said. "Long way from home, too."

"I'll trade you the investigation for the autopsy, if you want," I said coldly.

"Natural curiosity, Lieutenant," Murphy said cheerfully. "I figure he's been dead somewhere between eight to ten hours."

I checked my watch. "That brings it between midnight and two A.M. this morning."

6

The door swung open suddenly and Sergeant Polnik came lumbering in.

"I got a ride in the meatwagon, Lieutenant," he said breathlessly. "The Sheriff—" Then he got his first look at the guy on the bed and blinked rapidly. "Cheez!"

"What about the Sheriff?" I asked patiently.

"He said for you to get back to his office right away, only sooner." Polnik explained. "He was hopping mad like it was election year and you was running for Sheriff!"

"I'd like that," I said wistfully. "Sit around the County Sheriff's office all day making his secretary!"

"I never figured Miss Jackson was a girl like that?" Polnik sounded surprised.

"She isn't," I told him, "but I can dream, can't I?"

The boys from the meatwagon in their neat white coats filed through the doorway and the room got crowded suddenly.

"I only got here around a half-hour back," I said. "What's with Lavers—he's lost his mind again?"

"I wouldn't know, Lieutenant." Polnik shrugged helplessly. "But he sure wants you back in town in a hurry. Said for me to take over here."

"You can give me a ride in that miniature rocket of yours," Murphy interrupted. "Maybe prove my theory about guys that drive these foreign bugs?"

"Sports cars to you," I told him. "What theory?"

"They're all suffering from a guilt complex and it drives 'em into compulsive masochism," he said, his eyes gleaming enthusiastically. "Why else would they want to squeeze themselves into those bucket seats?"

Polnik stared down at the contents of Albert H. Marvin's billfold and grunted, "So he was a private eye, huh, Lieutenant?"

"The doc already said that," I grunted right back.

"Maybe he got hot? Knew too much about somebody so they knocked him off to shut him up?" Polnik theorized out loud. "What do I do, Lieutenant?"

I resisted the obvious answer, knowing he'd rather do anything but work. So I told him to go question the proprietor who had called in and reported the murder in the first place, then question the guests staying at the motel and find out if anyone had checked out this morning before the body was discovered.

Polnik's Cro-Magnon forehead corrugated deeply while he tried to memorize the instructions—I guessed I should have known better than try to tell him three things at the one time. That corpse must have unnerved me more than I'd realized.

I got back to the Sheriff's office just after eleven. His secretary, Annabelle Jackson—the blonde who's got everything but won't give one single inch—swiveled around in her chair and looked at me with an excited expression on her face.

"The Sheriff's been asking if you got back yet every five minutes, on the minute, for the last hour," she said breathlessly. "You'd better get in there fast!"

"So what's the panic?" I asked. "What's more important than a murder yet?"

"A quarter-billion dollars, I guess," she said, wide-eyed and still breathless.

"In fives and tens—and he wants me to help count it?"

"I mean the person who's in there with him right now is worth that much," Annabelle said. Her voice held a reverent tone as she breathed the name, "Mrs. Geoffrey Summers."

"She knocked over Fort Knox?" I said. "It's not our problem—that's to hell and gone over the county line.'

"I don't know how you got so dumb without even trying," she said fiercely. "You can't just stand there and tell me you've never heard of Mrs. Geoffrey Summers?"

"I never even heard of Mr. Geoffrey Summers," I admitted freely.

Annabelle took a sudden deep breath, not caring that she strained her blouse about as far as orlon cares to go, and that's a long, long way with a girl built the way she's built.

"Mrs. Summers is the New York socialite," she said rapidly. "Always makes the 'Ten Best Dressed' list every year. Her husband died three years back making her a widow and—"

"Leaving her a quarter-billion dollars along with the black weeds?" I finished for her. "I have the picture. If she was under fifty, I'd marry her, but even that much money is no consolation for spending the rest of my nights alongside a battle-ax—it can give a guy nightmares, I tell you!"

"Go on into the office, Al," Annabelle said sweetly. "You could be surprised."

The first surprise I got when I stepped into Sheriff Lavers' office was all the people in there already. Lavers is fat enough to make a crowd all by himself—add another three people and it's like a sellout at the ball game.

"What kept you?" Lavers asked with the open friendliness of a cornered cougar.

"Friction," I said. "The four wheels got to make continuous contact with the freeway and all that jazz."

"I hoped you'd show your usual disregard for the state speed limit," he said sourly. "I should have figured this was just business for you, not pleasure!"

With a quarter-billion dollars sitting right there in the room, I should worry about the County Sheriff. I gave the three visitors a lynx-eyed once-over, seeing if my years of training as a cop could help me spot the big money. I narrowed the candidates down to two right away—the third visitor was a man. I never heard of a guy yet calling himself "Mrs." Summers, even if they do tell me Greenwich Village is quite a place.

Lavers had a hunted look in his eyes as he turned toward the visitors. "This is Lieutenant Wheeler," he said. "Attached to my office from the Homicide Department on an indefinite basis, and an officer with considerable experience."

He studiously avoided looking at me while he made the build-up and I figured he must be in real trouble to make polite noises about and in front of me.

"Lieutenant," he continued quickly, "I'd like you to meet Mrs. Geoffrey Summers, who has a big problem."

"How do you do, Lieutenant," Mrs. Summers said with a slight touch of impatience in her voice.

So the money was the blonde and not the brunette. An elegant blonde somewhere in her late thirties and I dug

9

Annabelle's crack about me being surprised. Mrs. Summers was a slim, attractive blonde, and I wouldn't have minded spending some of my nights close to her if she was only worth two bits.

"Miss Brent, her attorney," Lavers continued.

"Lieutenant." The brunette nodded with a pleasant smile on her face. She could give her client between five and ten years, and the charcoal suit she wore would have looked businesslike if it hadn't been for the generous curves underneath.

"Mr. Hillary Summers," Lavers completed the introductions. "Mrs. Summers' brother-in-law."

Hillary Summers nodded vaguely and went back to what he'd been doing before—looking at nothing with his eyes open. He was a tall, lean guy, around forty, with black hair graying at the temples, and the kind of sensitive face a lot of women get instincts about—the kind of instincts they prefer to call maternal.

"Mrs. Summers," Lavers cleared his throat aggressively, "would you mind repeating to the Lieutenant your reasons for this visit?"

"Surely," she said.

She twisted her body slightly in the chair so she looked at me directly. Her eyes were a clear, deep blue and completely impersonal—she was talking to the hired help.

"This concerns my daughter Angela," she said crisply. "It's perfectly simple, Lieutenant. I have requested the Sheriff to take the correct and lawful action over the matter, but for some obscure reason he seems reluctant to do so."

"You just don't know who's a communist these days," I said sympathetically.

Miss Brent's lips twitched for a fraction of a second—about the same time it took for Mrs. Summers' face to get that bleak look.

"You find this amusing, Lieutenant?" she asked icily.

"No," I said. "Please go on."

"I live, of course, in New York," she said, wrapping up California in six words and dropping it neatly into the nearest paper-towel disposal unit. "Angela spent a year

10

at finishing school in Switzerland, returning six weeks ago. She's always been a wayward child and I'm afraid the year in Europe didn't change her. I lead a busy life of my own, and perhaps I didn't devote enough time to her after she got back."

She shrugged her shoulders gracefully. "To come to the point, Lieutenant, a week ago, she ran away with some nightclub singer from Greenwich Village called Rickie Willis. It's not only embarrassing, it's absurd! I hired a private detective to trace them, and at last he's found them. They are right here in Pine City, Lieutenant."

"That is," Miss Brent added pleasantly, "in the area of Sheriff Lavers' jurisdiction."

"Exactly," Mrs. Summers nodded. "So now I wish the Sheriff to take action—against this nightclub singer."

"For what—kidnaping?"

"I doubt if my daughter would agree that was the word," she said acidly. "They both need to be taught a sharp lesson, and I intend to see they get it!"

"How—exactly?" I asked.

"My daughter is seventeen and a half," she snapped. "I want you to arrest this man on a charge of statutory rape!"

I stared at her for a moment, then stared at Lavers, who rolled his eyes upward in an obvious appeal to the pagan god of county sheriffs to smite the woman where she sat.

"I understand the age of consent in California is eighteen," Mrs. Summers went on briskly. "Therefore, intimate relations with a minor is technically rape whether she was agreeable or not."

"That's right," I said. "But how will you prove it if your daughter won't testify?"

"I doubt if that will be a problem," she said acidly. "They're naturally registered as man and wife where they're staying, and I'm sure there won't be any difficulty in establishing the facts."

I lit a cigarette slowly and glanced at the female lawyer who shook her head slightly.

11

"This is not my advice, Lieutenant," she said evenly. "But Mrs. Summers is determined on this course of action."

"Isn't there also something called the Mann Act?" Mrs. Summers said coldly. "A federal law against transporting a minor across a state border for immoral purposes?"

"The FBI office is just four blocks down—" Lavers said in a hopeful rush of words that were chopped out in mid-sentence.

"I shall certainly see them if necessary," she told him. "But at this moment I want you, Sheriff Lavers, to take action against the man who's raped my daughter!"

"I side with Miss Brent," Hillary Summers said suddenly, in a soft, deep-timbred voice. "But my sister-in-law is determined this is the way to handle it. I've tried to impress her with the volume of publicity such an action will bring in its wake." He shuddered slightly. "The Press will have a field day with it—the daughter of Mrs. Geoffrey Summers, leader of New York society!"

"My daughter means more to me than the risk of cheap newspaper sensationalism!" Mrs. Summers snapped. "This is the only way to bring her to her senses!"

"You say this private detective you hired knows where they are now?" I asked her.

"He called me yesterday morning," she said, "and the three of us got on a plane right away. They're at a motel about fifteen miles south of here. A place called 'The Travelers' Rest,' or some equally ridiculous name."

After five seconds had ticked away, she shifted irritably in her chair.

"Really, Lieutenant! Must you stare at me like that?"

"This private detective you hired to find them," I said in a numbed voice. "His name was Marvin—Albert H. Marvin?"

"Why, yes. How did you know that?"

"Because I just got back from viewing his corpse," I told her. "Somebody pulped his skull with a hammer last night and I never saw anyone quite so dead as Albert H. Marvin in my whole life before!"

It was her turn to stare at me like that while the color ebbed slowly from her face and her mouth opened and framed words her paralyzed vocal cords wouldn't voice. Then her eyes glazed quickly and I caught her as she fell forward out of the chair.

·2·

I GOT BACK TO THE MOTEL JUST AFTER NOON AND FOUND Polnik in the manager's office. The manager was a stringy, gray-haired character who looked like he'd been cheating the mortician for the last ten years. He wore a faded blue shirt and a pair of crumpled gray pants and needed a shave from sometime yesterday morning.

"This is Mr. Jones, Lieutenant," Polnik told me. "He owns the place."

"How long you going to be fooling around here, Lieutenant?" Jones asked in a sour voice. "I got better things to do than stick around here all day answering fool questions."

"You could always try charging us rent," I told him. "Send the tab into the Sheriff's office." I looked at Polnik. "What did you find out?"

"Six of the cabins are rented," Polnik said. "I questioned all of the people in them and they don't know from nothing, never heard any unusual noise last night or anything like that. I got a list of their names and addresses."

"Anybody check out this morning early?"

"Yeah," he said, with a pleased expression on his face. "A couple—name of Smith!"

"Smith?" I repeated, and looked at the motel owner inquiringly.

"We get more Smiths!" he grunted. "Strictly one-

13

night rentals and they're always gone in the early morning, some of 'em before sunup even."

"What did these Smiths look like?"

"Young," Jones said laconically. "The guy was around twenty-five at most—acted tough like he'd been around and seen it all before."

He spat with methodical precision through the open window into the dust outside.

"The girl was real young—only a kid. Not that I got to see much of her, just a glimpse when she went by the office. She had black hair that needed a comb, and a mean look on her face like she was mad at something—I figured maybe she was one of these bootniks. She was wearing a man's shirt and a pair of jeans—tight jeans."

His eyes flickered for a moment, remembering. "Kids got no self-respect these days—just bums the lot of 'em —don't matter where they come from!"

"What time did they leave?" I asked patiently.

"I was up around seven and they were gone then," he said.

"What were they driving?"

"Looked like a new sedan," he said. "A drive-yourself, I'd guess."

"You remember the make—the license plates maybe?"

"I want to make like a cop in this business, Lieutenant, and I don't got no business," he said grimly. "Most of my trade come in to buy a night's privacy and no questions asked."

"Which cabin did you give them?"

"Seven."

"Marvin had nine," Polnik grunted. "What's with these Smiths?"

"Save it till later," I told him. Explaining the Smiths to the Sergeant would be a cinch—like explaining nuclear fission to a Pilgrim Father.

"When did they get here?" I asked Jones.

"Monday night around eight," he said. "They went straight to the cabin and like I told you, I only ever saw the girl the one time. They booked for two nights and the guy was out most of yesterday but the girl wasn't with

14

him. I went to bed around ten last night and he still wasn't back."

"When did Marvin arrive?"

"Monday night—maybe an hour after the Smiths checked in. He paid for one night, then yesterday morning he paid another night."

"Where's his car now?"

"Didn't have one," Jones sniffed. "Came in a cab."

"To a motel?" I said. "Didn't you figure that was kind of strange?"

"I been running this place the last ten years," he said simply. "There ain't nothing strange under the sun for me any more. If a guy checked in riding a camel I wouldn't be surprised!"

"Did the Smiths tell you they were leaving this morning?"

"No," he shook his head. "They just went."

"Did you talk to Marvin at all while he was here?"

"No. Only to give him a receipt for his money, that's all."

"Thanks," I said wearily. "You've been a great help."

"You going to get the hell out of here now?" he asked hopefully.

"You have my word, Mr. Jones," I assured him. "As soon as I possibly can!"

We took a look at the cabin the Smiths had rented and it was like the one Marvin had, but stripped clean with nothing left to show their stay—not even a squeezed-out tube of toothpaste. It looked like one hell of a case for clues.

I shoehorned Polnik into the passenger's seat of the Austin Healey and drove back into town again, taking time out at a diner for lunch on the way, wondering if Lavers would agree this was just the time for me to take my vacation.

It was around three when I got back inside his office—he was alone this time, chewing on a cigar with an air of morose expectancy like a cannibal sampling his first lean missionary.

"They weren't there," he said as soon as he saw me.

15

"Check," I agreed. "They were there—for two days, but they vanished around sunup this morning."

"It figures," he said. "No clues, of course?"

"They left in a sedan, the owner says," I told him. "A self-drive it looked like. With the things he doesn't see, this guy should be a cop!"

"The afternoon papers have got the story of the murder," Lavers said gloomily. "They don't have the tie-in with Mrs. Summers and her daughter yet, but they will!"

"You heard from the lab about the hammer?" I asked, and slid into one of the vacant visitor's chairs, facing him.

"No fingerprints." He chewed on the cigar some more. "I've asked New York for information on Marvin."

"How about Mrs. Summers?" I asked.

"She's staying at the Starlight Hotel—along with Miss Brent and her brother-in-law. You remember the news of Marvin's murder knocked her for a loop, but I've got a nasty feeling she'll recover fast and come howling after our blood again any minute!"

"You got to admire her maternal instincts," I said. "It's not every mother gets so all-fired anxious to prove her daughter's been raped—technically!"

"A lovely woman, Mrs. Summers," Lavers growled. "Reminds me of my mother-in-law. The first time she stopped nagging in fifty years, they called a mortician right away. She died with her mouth wide open. This doesn't get us anyplace, Wheeler, does it?"

"No, sir," I agreed.

"Don't you have any of your usual brilliant, free-wheeling ideas?"

"Yes, sir, Sheriff!" I said eagerly. "Is it O.K. with you if I take my vacation starting now?"

"Oh, sure," he snarled. "Just don't bother to come back—there won't be any reason for it!"

The desk clerk at the Starlight wore his usual supercilious look when he saw me.

"I'm afraid our rates would be a little too high for you, Lieutenant," he sniffed. "We do have a vacancy for a bellhop—do you hop?"

"You're kidding me again, Charlie," I said reproachfully. "I've come about the drains—or maybe it's just the hotel altogether—but people are complaining in the street and perfume sales are soaring throughout the city."

"You want to see one of our guests?" Charlie said with a faint shudder of distaste. "Flatfooted policemen treading all over our beautiful carpets! Which one?"

"You have more than one?" I said disbelievingly.

"One hundred and twenty-three, to be precise!"

"You must have the biggest con-game on the West Coast right here in Pine City," I said. "I want to see Miss Brent."

"She's in eight-oh-three," Charlie grunted. "If you wait a moment I'll call her and find out if she wants to see you."

"A room in this fleabag she may have," I said gently. "A choice about seeing me she hasn't."

"So all right already!" Charlie shrugged his shoulders with elaborate disdain. "The service elevator is at your disposal."

"I'll dispose with it right away," I told him. "Don't take any outdated credit cards, Charlie."

When I got there I found it wasn't a room, it was a suite—that figured with Mrs. Geoffrey Summers paying the tab one way or another. I knocked on the door and while I waited I daydreamed about getting Mrs. Summers mad at Charlie so she'd buy the hotel just for the pleasure of firing him—then rent me the place for a dollar a year. I'd have Lavers as doorman, dressed like a boy scout right down to the khaki shorts—Polnik as desk clerk— and I'd run a permanent harem in the penthouse suite with Annabelle Jackson as chief lady-who's-never-kept-waiting. . . .

"If it's amnesia, Lieutenant," a pleasant voice said, "be a doll and go have it on the next floor up."

My eyes started work again and the female lawyer, Miss Brent, came sharply into focus. She looked different from the way she'd looked in Lavers' office, one hell of a lot different. Her midnight-colored hair with the neat center part had somehow escaped the severe hair-do, and made a soft frame for her pixie face. The flecked hazel eyes held a warmer, nonlegal look, and her lips were

17

somehow softer, the lower lip stopping just short of a pout.

She'd discarded the efficient-looking charcoal suit for a black silk shirt that clung to the classic contours of her sharp-thrusting breasts, and a pair of mushroom wool-knit pants that fitted tight down to her ankles, creasing only where she creased.

"Any guy who'd waste time with amnesia when he could be talking to you would be crazy," I told her.

"Well, that's nice," she said in that voice with the husky overtone which did peculiar things to my spinal column. "You didn't come all the way over here just to tell me that, Lieutenant?"

"I figured we might talk a little?"

"A cozy chat?" Her lips curved in a mocking smile. "This is a new technique for a law officer, isn't it? I mean, you *are* working, Lieutenant, this is official business?"

"It started out that way," I said honestly. "Now you've got me confused."

"Maybe you'd better come in," she said, "and see my subpoenas."

I followed her into the living room of the suite and those wool-knit pants looked even tighter, rear view. She sat down in one of the armchairs and I sat opposite her.

"What's on your mind, Lieutenant?" she asked casually.

I told her what I'd found out when I went back to the motel—the "Smiths" who were Angela Summers and her singer boy friend, Rickie Willis, for sure. That they'd checked out early in the morning, and the way I saw it we didn't have much chance of finding them—they could be in Mexico by now.

"You'd have circulated a description of them and so on, Lieutenant?" she said. "Isn't there a good chance they'll be picked up?"

"I wouldn't put money on it," I said. "If they murdered Marvin, would they head for any place other than Mexico?"

"You think they killed him?"

"I can't think of any better suspects right now."

18

She relaxed in the chair, leaning her head back easily, but her eyes had lost that soft look and were guardedly watchful.

"This isn't why you came to see me, is it?" she said.

"No," I agreed. "I figured you'd like to know what's happened since Mrs. Summers passed out in the Sheriff's office this morning. Call it curiosity—a cop's curiosity—I hoped you might fill me in on the detail and background."

"You mean Lyn?"

"If that's Mrs. Geoffrey Summers, yes."

"Lyn's her Christian name," Miss Brent said. "She's also my client, Lieutenant, in case you've forgotten."

"Her interest in her daughter didn't sound motherly—or maybe I've got an old-fashioned approach," I said. "What's it all about?"

She lit a cigarette and looked at me for maybe five seconds before she answered.

"I guess it can't do any harm," she said finally. "Lyn is a widow, as you probably know. Her husband died three years back—they were a devoted couple and when he died something went out of her life forever—"

"The pocket handkerchief is brand new," I said anxiously. "You don't mind if I drop my tears on the carpet?"

"Not unless I have to swim out of here!" She grinned slowly. "I guess it did sound corny, at that—sorry. But it's true—the only thing she had left was Angela and I guess her daughter became an obsession with her. She's watched over the kid like a hawk and Angela's always needed watching—a wild one, Lieutenant! She was thrown out of four of the best private schools in the country by the time she was sixteen. The finishing school in Switzerland was a kind of last resort. Then she was thrown out of that."

"So she came back home, met Rickie Willis, and took off with him for parts unknown," I said.

"Lyn had plans for her," Miss Brent said evenly. "College in the fall—her coming-out party. The same kind of plans all mothers have maybe, except Lyn's would be on a much grander scale. High society is a delicate organism,

19

Lieutenant, but with wealth and prestige, Lyn could put Angela any place she wanted. She had the whole social season planned for her coming out—and after. The way she saw it, Angela would have a year, maybe a couple, in college—it wasn't terribly important how long. What was important was Angela's social success as the glittering daughter of Mrs. Geoffrey Summers, and her taking of New York society by storm. The high point being her marriage in the next two, three years to the right kind of eligible bachelor—an English title if it was old enough—a career diplomat maybe."

"And the way it turned out, it was a Greenwich Village nightclub singer," I said. "I can understand Mrs. Geoffrey Summers blowing her stack, but this statutory rape bit is carrying it to an extreme, isn't it?"

She smiled again, suddenly. "You don't understand the morality of the very rich, Lieutenant, that's your trouble!"

"Call me Al," I told her. "Don't let a client stand in the way of friendship."

"All right, Al," she said. "My name is Ilona, and a client of mine can stand in the way of anything, if necessary."

"You were telling me about the very rich, Ilona," I said. "To a guy who never had more than a thousand bucks at one time, it's fascinating."

"Angela has some money in her own right," Ilona said. "About three million dollars, but she doesn't get it until she's twenty-one. Right now she's still a minor under her mother's control, legally, and practically she has the two hundred dollars a month allowance Lyn gives her and nothing else. Lyn is desperate, Al. This is her last throw —if she loses, she knows she's lost her daughter for good. So she thinks the only way to make Angela listen to reason is to scare her so bad, she'll never even argue with her mother again."

"What about the publicity—the sensationalism?" I asked.

Ilona shrugged her shoulders and I marveled at the taut lift of her breasts under the silk shirt.

"It's a calculated risk. Lyn's own position is untouchable, and she thinks it will only be a seven-day sensation at the worst. Six months from now, the memory of the story will give Angela a certain glamor even, in high society. There are only two unforgivable sins with the international set, Al. One is to marry beneath your social position and the other, which is worse, is to lose your money!"

I lit myself a cigarette and thought about it for a while—it made sense in a mad kind of way, like a United Nations debate.

"I'll buy that," I said. "So when she got definite news of her runaway daughter and boy friend, she came hotfoot in pursuit bringing her lovely lawyer along for the ride. But why bring brother-in-law, too?"

"Hillary? He's taken the place of the man in the family ever since his brother's death. He advises Lyn on finance, handling the estate, and so on. In a crisis like this, I guess she thought Hillary should be along."

"She didn't take his advice, according to what he said this morning."

"Or mine for that matter," Ilona agreed. "Lyn can be a very determined woman when she wants. Imagine how frustrating it is to have more than enough money to buy anything that money can buy—then be faced with a situation where money is useless!"

"The only place I know where money's useless is Las Vegas," I said. "A weekend playing craps can be that kind of frustration."

"So," she smiled easily, "does that give you enough background and detail?"

"Almost," I said. "How about this private eye, Marvin? Did you hire him for Mrs. Summers, or was that her own idea?"

"It was Hillary's idea," she said. "He knew Marvin, said he was capable and discreet. I never even met him, and I'm almost sure Lyn didn't, either."

"Thanks a lot," I told her and got to my feet again. "You've been a big help."

"My pleasure." She stood up and walked to the door

with me. "I thought Pine City was going to be dull, but now I'm not so sure."

"I guarantee you'll be proved wrong," I assured her. "How's Mrs. Summers feeling now? She took the news about the murder pretty hard."

"She's still upset—or she was when I last saw her a couple of hours back," Ilona said. "I persuaded her to take a sedative and I hope she's sleeping now. You won't disturb her, will you?"

"I wouldn't dream of it," I said hastily. "If this morning was a demonstration of her usual relaxed approach, it would be me who got disturbed!"

Ilona smiled faintly. "You have to make allowances, Al—she was emotionally off balance."

"This afternoon she could've fallen overboard," I said. "I'm no headshrinker to throw her a lifeline."

· 3 ·

I GOT BACK TO MY APARTMENT AROUND SIX THAT EVE-ning and put a Peggy Lee record on the hi-fi machine because if anyone could soothe me right then it was Peggy. We're on a first names basis—natch—even if it is a strictly one-way deal. I know her from way back and she wouldn't know me from Hot Springs, Colorado.

After I'd left Ilona Brent at the Starlight Hotel, I'd spent a couple of hours back at the office without getting anyplace. The Sheriff had tossed a description of Angela Summers and Rickie Willis all over the country but nobody had found them yet. He kept on asking me didn't I have any ideas and I kept telling him that's right I didn't until the atmosphere got more explosive than Cape Canaveral and it looked like a good time for me to get the hell out of there, so I got.

I made a nice mellow drink to go along with Peggy's nice mellow voice and settled back in a chair to try and relax. If this was being a cop, I figured my old man was right and I should have gotten into a respectable racket like organizing a numbers game around the kindergarten set.

Halfway through the second drink the buzzer sounded, the squawking noise of a middle-aged spinster caught bending by a myopic Hollywood talent scout. I walked to the front door hoping this was the answer to my woman-less week and outside was a breathless blonde who'd just lost all her clothes in a hurricane and was seeking shelter for the next couple of months. Then I opened the door and there was a loud pinging noise as my dream sharply disintegrated.

Standing in the corridor was a guy around thirty with a nervous look on his face.

"Whatever you're selling, friend," I told him, "I either got it or don't want it."

"You're Lieutenant Wheeler?" he asked politely.

"Yeah," I said. "But it's still no sale."

"You're the officer in charge of the investigation into the private detective's murder out at that motel?"

"I could be his twin brother," I said cautiously. "Are you a process server?"

"My name's Willis," he said. "Ray Willis—I'm Rickie's brother."

"You know where he is—where the two of them are?" I asked rapidly.

"Sure," he said. "That's what I came to see you about."

The world was suddenly a beautiful place where undeserving cops get paid off anyway—like a Las Vegas in the sky. I grabbed hold of his arm in case he'd just disappear in a faint puff of smoke, then pulled him gently inside the apartment. I let go of him when we got into the living room and offered him a drink.

"Thanks, Lieutenant," he said gratefully. "I could sure use one."

I made him a drink, revitalized my own, then took another look at him. He was a nice-looking guy in a cheap kind of way with thick glossy black hair and a thin mustache. His eyes were heavy-lidded and never kept still, like an appliance salesman always looking for the nearest exit once he's got the signature on the dotted line and the customer hasn't had time to read the fine print yet. His clothes were expensive but he was a razor-sharp dresser and it put your teeth on edge just looking at him for more than five seconds at one time.

"We heard about it on the radio," he said, then gulped down half the contents of his glass. "So we flew right back to Pine City."

"Where from—Tijuana?"

"Mexico?" He shook his head blankly. "Nevada, Lieutenant."

"Where's your brother and the girl now?"

"In a downtown hotel," he said nervously. "Not booked in under their right name, of course. I figured the best thing was to see you first and find out what happened."

"This guy Marvin got himself murdered two cabins down from the one they had last night at the motel," I snarled. "That's what happened—didn't they mention that minor detail on the radio?"

He drained the glass before he answered. "Well, sure they did, Lieutenant. But Rickie and Angela never had nothing to do with it, and that's the truth."

"Then they don't have a thing to worry about," I said. "You'd better take me to them."

"O.K.," he nodded. "I just didn't want to get them involved with the newspaper guys and everything right off —that's why I didn't take them straight to the sheriff's office."

"What are you—their keeper?"

His mouth twitched into a semblance of a grin. "Well, I'm Rickie's older brother, Lieutenant, and I guess he kind of looks to me for advice when he's in any trouble."

"O.K.," I said. "Let's go find out just how much trouble he's got."

The hotel was four blocks, and at the same time a million light-years, away from the Starlight. Some guy with the same type humor as that motelkeeper had called it the Grand. A seedy-looking dump with the paint job faded and peeling—a last resort for crapped-out traveling salesmen and out-of-work, aging actresses. The kind of joint where they'd rent you a room by the hour.

Ray Willis shrugged apologetically as we got out of the car and walked across the sidewalk into the lobby.

"They're short of folding money, Lieutenant," he said softly. "This is all they can afford."

The furnishings were shabby, dusty—matching the desk clerk who didn't look like he was getting his fair share of the wages of sin. It figured. In this kind of decay there could be neither vice nor pleasure in sin—only habit could keep it going. We rode the wheezing elevator to the third floor, then Willis led the way down the corridor to a room marked 301, and knocked twice.

A younger edition of himself opened the door abruptly and stared sullenly at us.

"Rickie," Ray Willis said quickly, "I brought the Lieutenant along with me."

Rickie Willis took a good look at me and his eyes said he didn't care much for what he saw. It was a mutual feeling—he was tougher as well as younger than his brother. His black hair was chopped into a bristling crewcut and he was a real blunt dresser compared to Ray—he wore a tired, almost shapeless sports coat in large red-flecked checks, and a pair of creased cotton pants. The green knitted shirt underneath was open at the neck far enough to show the black wiry hair that sprouted on his chest like he gave it a hormone shot before breakfast every day.

"You tell him we didn't have nothing to do with it, man?" he asked in a thick-timbred voice.

"I figured you should tell him that, Rickie," Ray said in a soothing voice. "Ask us in, will you?"

"Uh—sure," Rickie said. "Hey, Angel!" he called over his shoulder. "You decent? We got company—cops no less!"

He waited a couple of seconds, got no answer, shrugged his wide shoulders under that refugee-from-vaudeville coat, and opened the door wider. I walked past him into the room with Ray following me, and Rickie closed the door behind us.

The two single beds proved the wages of sin were a lumpy mattress if nothing more. There was a square yard of carpet, frayed at the edges, on the floor between the two beds; a beat-up dressing table with two dirty glasses and a near-new fifth of bourbon on the top completed the furnishings. The girl was standing directly under the harsh light from the naked lightbulb, a cigarette dangling from the corner of her mouth, watching me with a bland expression on her face.

She was a brunette with a bird's-nest hair-do sitting like an inverted cone on top of her head. Her eyes were enormous, matching the color of her hair, and they had a veiled, negative look in them as she watched me.

Nobody would call her pretty even, but there was something about that oval face with the high cheekbones, small tiptilted nose, and soft moist mouth with the almost ridiculous kewpie-doll heart shape, that did things to you. Then you looked at her body and knew right away that the face was the teaser—the hook. The figure was perfection you'd never believed possible before—not even in the girdle ads.

She wore a crew-necked orlon sweater in a bright lemon color which must have been three sizes too small, the way it molded the swelling, pointed perfection of her arrogant breasts—close enough to prove beyond doubt that she wore nothing at all underneath. Along with the orlon sweater, she wore black stretch-nylon tights that were stretched to the limit, giving her that bare look that nakedness can't ever match. If she wore anything underneath those tights, I didn't believe it because nobody's come up with a fabric lighter than air yet.

"Angela," Ray's voice broke the silence, "this is Lieutenant Wheeler."

"Don't spoil his dreams, Ray," she said in a mock-serious, little girl's voice. "He's not finished yet."

Somehow my throat was dry and I had to clear my voice before I could speak. "You're Angela Summers?" I asked the obvious question.

"Little orphan Angela, that's me," she said, mimicking my flat, official voice. "I thought the 'Dragnet' technique was old hat now, Lieutenant—or hasn't anyone told you yet?" Her voice tried hard to be tough but even on her, all that education couldn't have been entirely wasted, and some of the cultured accents kept coming through.

"You want to play this cute, we can go down to the Sheriff's office and start over," I told her.

"Take it easy, Angela!" Ray said in an agonized voice. "You got enough troubles already."

She walked over to the nearest bed and the springs chimed harshly as she plumped down onto it. Then she crossed her legs daintily, hugging one knee with both hands while she looked up at me with an expression that was an equal mixture of polite expectancy and open derision.

"Yes, Lieutenant?" she asked in a demure voice.

Rickie Willis slouched across to the dressing table, sloshed neat bourbon into one of the dirty glasses, then carried it across to the bed and sat down beside the girl.

"We never had nothing to do with the septic eye getting himself liquidated!" he said fiercely. "Man, we never knew he was for real even—no contact. You dig?"

"Why don't we get original and take it from the beginning—from when you lit out of New York a week back?" I suggested wearily.

Rickie shrugged again and I wondered if that woolknit shirt was fazing some skin allergy or maybe it was just the hair on his chest limbering up.

"It was a drag, man!" he muttered. "We ride the railroad to Chi and give the jazz joints a quick going over but that was Dullsville—and a pad under the El! Who can sleep in a joint that's jumping all night? So next day we fade onto the rails again to L.A."

"We stayed in a downtown hotel in Los Angeles for two days, Lieutenant," Angela said sweetly. "Then we got tired of it, so Rickie got a drive-yourself car and we just drifted around—spent the next night at a motel in Santa Monica. About then we realized we were almost out of money, so we came into Pine City to see Ray. We thought he could help us."

"You stayed two nights at the motel and checked out early this morning," I said. "Marvin picked you up at Santa Monica and followed you into Pine City—he got

27

into that motel just one hour after you did. And you never saw him, not even once, during the whole three days?"

"Maybe we did," Angela said innocently. "How do we know? We didn't know who he was anyway." She put her hand on Rickie's thigh and squeezed it affectionately. "We didn't exactly have much time for other people, Lieutenant. I'm sure you know what I mean."

I looked at Ray Willis because if I looked at those stretched nylon tights any longer I was going to bust a blood vessel, and who needs a coronary when we got taxes already?

"Where do you fit?" I asked him.

"The first I knew about it was when Rickie called me yesterday morning, Lieutenant," he said anxiously. "After he told me what it was all about, I suggested he'd better come and see me so we could talk. He came over to my apartment around four or five yesterday afternoon and stayed late—maybe midnight when he left."

"You sure of the times?" I asked.

He glanced at his brother for a moment, then shook his head. "Not real sure, Lieutenant, no. Maybe it was ten-thirty, eleven. We never had a reason to check."

"So you see now, Lieutenant," Angela said in the same sweet but crisp voice. "We know nothing about the poor man's murder!"

"I'd like to believe that," I told her. "Along with the long line of concidence that's shaped up into circumstantial evidence already!"

"That's plain stupid!" Angela said coldly. "A sad little man peeping through keyholes for a living—why should we bother to kill him? What harm could he do us?"

"He located you for your mother," I said. "She was in the office this morning raising all kinds of hell because we wouldn't go right out and book your boy friend for statutory rape."

For a split second she wasn't going to believe it, then her mouth curled slowly.

"Dear, darling Mom!" she said softly. "The girl with the new approach. If she wasn't all twisted up inside with a brain like an overripe peach crawling with maggots, she

28

should have known if anyone had a justifiable plea for rape it would be Rickie, not me!"

"It's a technical offense," I explained. "Eighteen is the age of consent in California, and you're not eighteen yet."

She pulled a face at Rickie, then her fingers darted inside his shirt suddenly and plucked a hair from his chest, making him yelp sharply.

"You big, masterful brute, you!" she said fondly. "Taking advantage of a little kid like me!"

"Her own daughter!" Ray Willis said solemnly. "Can you imagine that? What kind of a woman is she?"

"The usual kind—as far as I could see," I snarled at him. "Where's the phone?"

"Down the hall—you need a dime," Rickie grunted. "What's with the phone?"

"I'll call the Sheriff's office and have them send a car," I said. "We wouldn't all fit in mine."

"Are you arresting us, Lieutenant?" Angela gave me the wide-eyed look.

"No," I told her. "Just taking you in for further questioning—once your mother sees you, she might change her mind about that statutory rape bit."

"Oh, I think she will, Lieutenant," Angela smiled confidently. "In fact, I don't think she has a choice."

"How's that?" I said cautiously.

"Well"—her shoulders moved gracefully under the orlon sweater and the twin peaks moved in unison with them— "I don't think you can prosecute a husband on those grounds, can you?"

"Husband!" I pointed at Rickie disbelievingly. "Him?"

"We were married at eleven this morning," she said easily. "Why else do you think we flew to Nevada?"

I turned my head slowly and glared at Ray Willis. "Your advice?" I asked in a choked voice.

His eyes cringed for a moment, then he got that righteous look on his face again.

"What else could I tell them, Lieutenant?" He gestured pleadingly with both hands held palm-up. "The way things were between them I didn't figure it was right them not being married!"

· 4 ·

POLNIK BROUGHT THE CAR AND HIS EYES BUGGED WHEN he saw Angela in all her stretched-nylon glory. He only got one look as she climbed into the back of the car but that was enough—the red lights had to look after themselves all the way back to the office.

When we got there, I left him with them in the outer office while I disappeared into the inner sanctum and gave the Sheriff a fast run-down on what had happened.

Lavers had been home when I called in and from the look on his face, his dinner was still there on the table, untouched.

"They got married in Nevada this morning," he repeated slowly when I'd finished telling him. "Oh, brother! Won't Mrs. Geoffrey Summers love that!"

"She'll have to dream up a new gimmick," I agreed. "Is the marriage legal, I wonder?"

"In Nevada anything's legal so long as you buy a license first," he grunted. "I called her mother as soon as I got back to the office—she'll be here any minute."

"What do you figure on doing with the newlyweds?" I asked him. "We don't have a thing to hold them on, Sheriff."

"Material witnesses," he grunted, but he didn't sound very sure.

"You can hold them for twenty-four hours maybe," I said. "Don't forget Momma Summers will have her tame lawyer along."

He glared at me, his face reddening rapidly. "Don't

you have one little piece of evidence, Wheeler? Just something small—not conclusive even—we can use?"

"Not one," I said cheerfully. "But remember, Sheriff, the darkest hour is before the dawn—or haven't you ever left a warm bed to go home?"

"This isn't the time to make lousy jokes, Wheeler!" he grated. "If we don't pin this murder on somebody fast, I'll be laughed out of office on every front page throughout the whole country!" He bared his teeth at me. "And I'll make sure you come along for the ride!"

"You know something, Sheriff?" I said wistfully. "It's not the money that keeps me going, it's your faith."

"I'd better take a look at them," he rasped, and eased his paunch out from behind the desk so it drooped sharply with no visible means of support.

We got back into the outer office and Lavers nodded curtly to the Willis brothers when I introduced him, then took his first look at Angela. I waited for the steam to erupt out of the top of his head. He gurgled helplessly for a few seconds, then swung round toward me, his face an ugly, mottled color.

"Wheeler!" he thundered. "Why the hell didn't you wait for her to get dressed before you brought her back to the office?"

"I am dressed, you dirty old man," Angela said calmly, "and don't look at me like that again—my husband doesn't care for it!"

The only thing that saved Lavers from a ruptured ulcer right then was the arrival of Mrs. Geoffrey Summers, her lawyer, and her brother-in-law. Mrs. Summers swept into the office to the sound of invisible trumpets with the other two following in her wake like respectful courtiers. She stopped a couple of feet away from the chair her daughter occupied and surveyed her with a clinical eye.

"You look disgusting!" she observed coldly. "Prancing around in your underwear—don't you have any modesty at all?"

"Heck, Mom!" Angela grinned at her nastily, burlesquing the junior high drawl. "You know how it is after you've been stat-raped—the little things in life don't seem so important any more."

Mrs. Summer's face lost color fast. She opened her mouth to say something else, then changed her mind and closed it with a snap.

"Well, Sheriff?" She lanced him with a steely gaze. "You have no further excuses to procrastinate now— you've got the man responsible right here in your office. Arrest him!"

"For gosh sakes, Mom," Angela accentuated the maddening drawl even further. "Don't get so excited—you haven't even heard my big news yet."

Mrs. Summers ignored her daughter icily while she waited for Lavers to do something dramatic. From the look on his face the only hope she had right then was a sudden and spectacular heart seizure.

"It's about Rickie and me," Angela said brightly, "and I just know you'll want to be the first to congratulate us, Mom. I mean, golly! Gee willikins! and all that kind of jazz, we got married this morning."

For a while there I figured Mrs. Geoffrey Summers had gone into a trance. Her eyes closed slowly and she just stood there, her whole body rigid.

"It's not true?" she whispered finally. "It can't be."

"I got the marriage certificate right here in my pocket," Rickie Willis said sullenly. "You can X-ray it, if you want!"

"Look at it this way, Mom," Angela simpered. "You haven't lost a daughter—you've gained a son. Rickie!"

"Yeah?" he queried.

"Give your new mom a great big kiss!" she said happily. "I just know you two will get along fine together— be a couple of real pals—natch!

Mrs. Summers had her eyes open again and I saw them start to glaze over—and for the second time since we'd met I stepped forward and caught her just before she hit the floor. It was getting monotonous. I eased her into an armchair, and Ilona Brent took over from there.

Hillary Summers walked over to where Rickie stood, his face pale and drawn.

"Let me see that certificate," he said curtly.

"Who're you?" Rickie growled at him.

"He's your Uncle Hillary, sweetie," Angela said. "Don't

speak rudely to him, he may bust out crying. He's the sensitive type—does a lot of social work among the high school set and I guess that's what makes him sensitive."

Rickie fumbled in his pocket, then pulled out a folded document and handed it to Summers. After he'd glanced through it rapidly, Hillary took it across to Ilona.

"Is this the real thing?" he asked jerkily.

Ilona studied it for a moment, then shook her head doubtfully. "I'm not certain—it would have to be checked," she said. "At any rate, she would have had to lie about her age—you have to be eighteen in Nevada the same as here to get married without consent."

"Then it's not binding?" Hillary said.

"I don't know off hand. It depends on the Nevada law —whether it actually says such a marriage is illegal."

Lavers gave a rasping cough which drew attention to himself, and it was about time. "I'm not concerned with the legality of their marriage!" he snarled. "I'm concerned with a murder—or have you all forgotten that already?"

"You've had both of them in your hands for the last two hours or so," Ilona said sharply. "Haven't you finished questioning them yet?"

"I haven't even started," Lavers grunted. "Now the touching family reunion is over, I'd like the three of you to get out of my office and let me get on with my job."

Mrs. Summers must have had the recuperative powers of an ox. Suddenly she sat bolt upright in the chair, pushing Ilona's helping hand away from her impatiently.

"I think that is an excellent idea," she said briskly. "We shouldn't discourage Sheriff Lavers from doing his duty—it's taken him all this time to make up his mind to start already. We'll leave now."

Ilona hesitated for a moment. "You'll want me to represent Angela, of course?"

"I want no such thing!" Mrs. Summers said curtly. "She got herself into this mess, she can get herself out." She stood up, adjusting the blue mink wrap around her shoulders. "It must be obvious to you, Ilona, as well as me. Once he"—she nodded in Rickie's direction briefly —"knew Marvin had found them, he had to do something desperate, so he killed Marvin to keep him quiet.

33

Then in panic he rushed Angela off to Nevada and married her. It worked both ways, don't you see? Anyone knows a wife can't testify against her husband, and he made it harder for us to get rid of him, too."

"You out of your mind?" Rickie blinked at her. "What's the deal? The way you talk to Angie, I'd figure you'd be glad to get rid of her this way."

"If you think," she hissed at him venomously, "that you will blackmail me for one red cent even, you're badly mistaken, Mr. Whatever-your-name-is! I don't have to raise my little finger to be rid of you because the courts will do that for me. You'll go to the gas chamber for murdering that unfortunate little private detective, and inside a year from now, Angela will be a widow!"

Rickie looked at his brother numbly. "What's with this broad?" he mumbled. "I don't dig her jive, man. How come she keeps spilling acid over my face all the time?"

"She's sick, Rickie," Ray said in a consciously pious voice. "Sick up here." He tapped the side of his head with one finger. "You should feel sorry for her, she needs help."

A volcanic rumble came from Lavers. "So help me, Wheeler!" he said in a rising voice. "If you don't get the three of them out of here in the next ten seconds I'll book them for obstructing justice!"

"Really, Sheriff!" Ilona laughed shortly. "You couldn't possibly—"

"All right then!" Lavers bellowed. "Obstructing traffic! Trespass! You got five seconds left!"

Polnik opened the door for them, that goggle-eyed expression still fixed on his face.

"I think it would be better if we left," Hillary said, and took Mrs. Summers' arm, leading her toward the door. Ilona followed them, with Lavers waiting at the boil until the door closed behind them. Polnik stared at him blankly.

"Get a female officer to look after this girl!" Lavers told him. "You'd better come into my office, Wheeler, and bring that—" he stared at Rickie for a moment, "—husband with you!"

Two hours later we were no further than when we'd started. Both Angela and Rickie stuck to their original story, which was simple enough. They hadn't known who Marvin was, they'd never noticed him around anyplace, including the motel. Rickie had gone to his older brother for advice because he was worried about what Angela's mother might do about her running away with him. He knew—I quote—she hated Angela's guts and would do anything to break them up. His brother had given him good advice if obvious—marry the girl—so that's what he did.

Ray Willis had backed up his story with that phony do-good look on his face that made the back of my hand twitch every time I saw it.

Lavers lit a cigar but his heart wasn't in it and the smoke only limped across the desk toward me.

"What have we got?" he said miserably. "Nothing!"

"No word from New York on Marvin yet?"

"Nor Rickie Willis either," he grunted. "Maybe we should get the girl back and go through it one more time."

"I had you figured for a lot of things, Sheriff," I said wonderingly, "but never a masochist."

"You got any better ideas?"

"Big brother," I said. "He's out of character—he must have an angle."

"Like what?" the Sheriff asked bleakly.

"There I give up," I admitted. "He plays piano in a downtown club—he says—has a room there."

"It figures," Laver said. "The other one is a singer— why shouldn't Ray play the piano?"

"No reason," I said. "I might go watch him play for a while—I could get lucky and see the piano lid drop at the wrong time, maybe take off all his fingers at the wrist. I'd like that."

"Get the girl back in here," Lavers said tiredly. "Let's get this over with so I can go home and cut my throat."

The woman officer brought Angela back in and sat beside her silently. She was a redhead in the full flush of first or maybe second girlhood, but under that heavy blue uniform you couldn't tell.

Angela's mouth drooped at the corners and the bottom lip had a definite pout.

"What is this?" she demanded angrily. "The third degree or something?"

"Don't tempt me!" Lavers muttered. "No, Miss—"

"Mrs. Willis," she corrected him coldly.

"Mrs. Willis—we just want to ask you some more questions, that's all."

"Don't you ever run out of questions?" she snapped. "Are you getting payola for this or something?"

"Answer the jackpot question, Angela, and we can all go home," I said.

"How many times do I have to say it?" she said stormily. "I don't know who killed him—I never even met him!"

"He was hired to find you and Willis," Lavers said in a tired voice. "He caught up with you in Santa Monica, we know—maybe in L.A. even? He stayed right on your tail into Pine City, had a cabin two down from yours. Yesterday morning he called your mother in New York and told her where you were and—"

"Hold it!" Angela said. "When did dear old Mom get here?"

"She got a plane right after his call," I said.

"With Hillary—and the Brent woman?"

"I guess so."

Lavers snorted impatiently. "Don't sidetrack the question, Mrs. Willis! The only reason Marvin had for being in that motel was you and your husband! You're the only two people who could have any possible motive for killing him, and—"

"You're wrong, Sheriff," she said softly, "but so wrong!"

"The guy that owns the motel maybe didn't like the color of Marvin's socks, so he beat in his head?" Lavers asked with heavy sarcasm.

"You are three suspects short," she said. "If they flew over right after Marvin called yesterday morning they would have been here by late afternoon at least, wouldn't they?"

"Sure, but—"

"Have you checked them out yet, Sheriff?" she asked tensely. "How do their alibis stack up? And I do mean dear old Mom, and Uncle Hillary—bless his sensitive little hands—and not forgetting the legal eagle with the cute feathers!"

"What possible reason could any of them have for murdering Marvin!" Lavers growled.

"That's for you to find out!" Angela said tartly. "But they could have—they were right here in this little hick town of yours, weren't they?"

Lavers buried his face in his hands for a suffering moment. "Get her out of here before I lose what's left of my mind!" he groaned. "I can't take any more tonight."

"No reason to hold them, sir?" I asked politely.

"Not yet—but make sure they stay right where we can find them and don't get any bright ideas about taking a long trip suddenly."

"Yes, sir," I said. "Anything else?"

He took his hands away from his face for a moment to scowl at me. "Wheeler, I'm getting to be an old man fast, but I've always treated you right, haven't I?"

"There are two ways of looking at it, Sheriff," I said thoughtfully. "From my point of view the answer's no— but then I guess we have to consider your point of view?"

"Did I ever ask you a favor?"

"Not since yesterday that I remember."

"Then I'm asking one small favor from you now, Wheeler. If you haven't come up with anything by morning—turn yourself in and confess?"

"Can you guarantee a promotion if I play ball?" I asked eagerly.

"I can guarantee some new faces around this office if we don't get some results in the next twenty-four hours," he said. "If you've got any spare time, Wheeler, you might try thinking up some new routines for us."

"Routines?" I said blankly.

"I was thinking a song and dance act would be better than starving to death," he said gloatingly. "And I've seen you go through a dozen different routines right here in this office!"

· 5 ·

RAY WILLIS SAT BESIDE ME IN THE HEALEY WITHOUT saying anything and it looked like another routine that was getting monotonous.

"The club's in the next block?" I asked him as we crossed an intersection.

"About halfway down, Lieutenant," he said coldly. "I appreciate you taking the trouble to drive me."

"It was nothing, Ray," I said warmly. "I guess you got a long night ahead of you, playing piano and all. I just figured if I could help you out a little, I should. You helped your brother, giving him that good advice—so now I help you. We all help each other and it makes the world go round and never mind the squares."

"Here," he grated.

I stopped the Healey at the curb and looked across the sidewalk at the plain wooden door with two big brass rings attached to the center panel.

"This is the most discreet nightclub I ever did see, Ray," I told him. "No neon, even?"

"It's a key club, Lieutenant."

He eased himself out of the car quickly. "Thanks again for the ride. Good night."

"Not so fast!" I got out my side and walked around to join him on the sidewalk. "You don't think I'm going home now without even hearing you play the piano?"

He forced a smile onto his lips while his eyes held a warm, murderous gaze. "Well, that would be real nice, Lieutenant, but I'm afraid it's not possible. Like I said, it's a key club—private, you know? Each member has his own key and they're only allowed to bring guests three nights a week, and this just isn't one of those nights. I'm sorry."

"Don't be." I patted his shoulder encouragingly. "It so happens I'm the owner of one of the most exclusive credit cards in the whole country—gets me in any place."

"Yeah?" he said dismally.

"Sure." I smiled happily. "So there's no problem about me getting in with you, Ray. I'll just produce my credit card. *Cop-carte blanche,* they call it."

He turned toward the door and fished a key out of his pocket. Ray was a tryer but he knew when it was smart to quit. We went inside where there was subdued light, thick carpet, and a tinkling piano somewhere in the background.

"That's a break, Ray," I said. "They got somebody pinch-hitting for you tonight."

A stunning blonde in sequined black bra and tights suddenly materialized in front of us. She had the longest legs I'd ever seen outside of my dreams; encased in black mesh nylons, they were the sexiest legs I'd ever seen, too.

"Good evening, Mr. Willis," she said in a husky voice. "May I take your hat?"

"Yeah," he said morosely.

"You can take mine, too," I told her earnestly. "Wear it in good health."

She smiled warmly at me. "Welcome to Club Double Zero, sir. Any friend of Mr. Willis is always welcome. I'll take good care of your hat."

A beefy character in a tight dinner jacket pushed his way through the drapes that separated us from the rest of the club, and the small foyer got suddenly crowded.

"Hey!" he said anxiously. "Where you been all night, Ray? I told you last week that redhead—Tina—was a lush. Boy! You should have seen her earlier tonight—started to tear the joint apart, chair by chair. Before we gave her the rush she hauled off and gave old man Denby a black eye. Was he mad! Yelling his head off the place wasn't run right and what the hell did the owner mean by not even being here when there was trouble. You'd better talk to him, Ray, he—"

"Shut up!" Ray snarled at him.

"I said something?" The beefy guy looked bewildered. "We got big trouble you don't want to know about it?"

"Why would it worry the piano-player?" I asked mildly.

He stared at me for a moment. "Piano-player?" He wheezed suddenly and his whole body shook in undulating spasms. "Yeah—that's rich, I like that! Why would it worry the piano-player! Ray, how's about introducing me to your friend?"

"This is Lieutenant Wheeler," Ray said slowly, with icicles forming over each word. "From the County Sheriff's office."

The beefy character stopped laughing—like that. I watched the apple in his throat leap up and down like a demented elevator until I got tired of it.

"You made a boo-boo, pal?" I asked gently.

"Excuse me," he said jerkily. "I just remembered a couple of things I got to—" He fumbled his way blindly through the drapes and disappeared again.

I lit a cigarette leisurely, then looked at Ray's set face.

"Fancy piano-player," I said cheerfully.

"So I've got a piece of the club," he said tightly. He held up his hand with the thumb and forefinger almost touching. "A very little piece, Lieutenant. Is that a crime?"

"Who was the fat guy with the sense of humor?"

"That's Joe Diment, the club manager."

"The way he talked, I figured you had all the pieces, Ray," I said.

"That Joe," he whispered. "The loud-mouthed bum!"

"I can't wait to see your piano, Ray," I said. "Why don't we go on in?"

He hesitated for a moment, then shrugged his shoulders helplessly. "Maybe we'd better go into my office," he said.

"You play your piano in an office?" I queried.

"O.K.! O.K.!" He clenched his teeth. "The piano-playing bit is just a hobby—I own the club!"

"You see, Ray?" I said encouragingly. "Right there you

40

were honest and it didn't hurt one little bit, did it? Why should I care anyway?"

He pushed the drapes aside and I followed him into the main room of the club. The lights were even more subdued inside than they were in the foyer. A bar, with the impressive line-up of brands discreetly displayed by indirect light, ran almost the length of one wall. There was a small dance floor right next to the tinkling piano, and the rest of the place was taken up with tables and the people who sat around them.

The Double Zero looked like it was doing good business—I never saw so many middle-aged guys and young dolls in one place before. I counted three cigarette girls as we walked across the room, all of them wearing the same kind of sequined outfit the hatcheck girl wore, except the colors were different. There was one brunette in a white bra and tights that made me feel like a real Marlboro man and I didn't care if the tattooing did hurt.

In the far corner was an ornate, heavy-timbered staircase, and just beside it, a door with nothing on it to indicate whether a lady had guessed right or not. Ray opened the door and I followed him inside into an office, which proved I'd guessed wrong.

Joe Diment, the guy with the beef and misplaced sense of humor, was standing at the bar beside the king-sized executive desk. He put his glass down quickly on the bartop as we came in.

"I needed something for my nerves, Ray," he said quickly. "After shooting off my mouth like that. Cheez! How stupid can I get?"

"You already demonstrated that," Ray told him.

He walked across the room to the bar, and stopped a couple of feet away from Diment, facing him.

"Hell! I'm sorry, Ray." Diment sounded nervous. "But how was I to know?"

"Never mind!"

"Well, O.K." Diment tried to smile. "I hate to bother you again, Ray, but that Denby guy is still squawking his head off upstairs—he's still sore about that redhead. I can't do nothing with him—he figures for the kind of dough he's paying we ought to spot a lush before she

41

can get close enough to black his eye when he's only looking for what he already paid—"

Ray backhanded him across the mouth with brutal force and Diment rocked back on his heels, his eyes closed tight.

"That big mouth of yours, Joe," Ray whispered. "It'll be the death of you one of these days!"

Then he backhanded him twice more with careful deliberation. I watched the tears flow down the beefy guy's face, mingling with the blood that trickled from his cut upper lip.

"Get out of here, Joe," Ray told him. "My insides start heaving, just looking at you."

Diment opened his eyes again slowly. "I finish the drink first, Ray?" he asked in a cracked voice.

Ray picked up the glass and threw the contents into his face. Diment whimpered softly as the liquor splashed against his eyeballs, and he groped for his pocket handkerchief with clawing fingers.

"Now you finished your drink, Joe," Ray told him. "You can go, huh?"

The fat boy stumbled past me toward the door, dabbing his eyes gently with the fine linen handkerchief as he went. A moment later the door closed behind him gently, and I wondered if he was heading straight for the employment agency.

Willis stood with his back toward me without moving for a little while; then he moved into the bar and set up a couple of glasses.

"Drink, Lieutenant?" he asked without any inflection in his voice at all.

"Scotch on the rocks, a little soda," I said.

I moved over to a comfortable-looking armchair close to the desk and relaxed into it while he made the drinks, then brought them across to the desk with him. He sat behind the desk and raised his glass. "Let's drink to that credit card of yours, Lieutenant. It sure gets you into the most intimate situations!"

"What could you expect—with that big, fat double-zero right on your front door?" I asked him. "What's upstairs?"

"Living space," he said. "I've got a couple of rooms. Diment and a couple of the other guys got a room up there, too."

"I'll use my credit card if you want," I said. "Maybe I could be a help, Ray? Smooth-talk old man Denby for you—the guy who paid for a redhead and got a black eye instead. You remember him, don't you—the guy Joe Diment couldn't forget?"

He lit a cigarette then looked at me with bleak eyes. "O.K.," he snapped in a crisp voice. "You've got the ball—what now?"

"I like you better this way," I told him sincerely. "Being your real self, Ray, slapping guys around and throwing liquor in their faces. It goes better with high-class pandering than that boy-scout act you've been pulling down at the Sheriff's office all evening."

"So?"

"So this club of yours doesn't interest me that much," I said. "It's inside the city limits and I work for the county sheriff's office. The city vice detail would be most interested, naturally, but me—I'm interested in finding out who killed this Marvin guy."

"I wish I could help, Lieutenant," he said flatly. "But I've already told you what I know, and that isn't much."

I tasted the drink and like I'd expected, it was very good Scotch.

"Where were you last night around midnight?" I asked.

"Right here in the club," he said promptly.

"Can you prove that?"

"If I have to—there were plenty of people around who saw me. You don't think I knocked off the peeper!"

"It's an interesting thought," I said. "You have a record, Ray?"

"No."

"I can check it with no trouble," I told him.

"The answer's still no."

"How about the kid brother?"

He finished his drink in one quick gulp, then lowered the glass carefully onto the desktop like he expected it to disintegrate in his hand.

43

"This I can check—we're waiting for an answer from New York right now," I added.

"Rickie did two years a while back," Ray said thinly. "He was only a kid, just got himself in with the wrong gang."

"How long back?"

"Three years maybe?"

"That makes him twenty-two at the time," I said cleverly. "But maybe he took a long time growing?"

"So he made a mistake, got caught, and served his time," Ray said. "You going to hold it against him the rest of his life?"

"I don't know yet," I snarled. "I'm getting tired of sitting around all night with a two-bit bordello-keeper and getting no place. I want the truth out of you, Willis, the real reason why your kid brother came to see you last night, and this is your last chance to tell it!"

He rubbed his chin nervously, the stubby fingers gouging into the flesh.

"He was worried sick," he said quickly. "Didn't know what to do. He met this Summers kid in the Village joint where he was working. She was all over him like a rash and—"

"They were both on the make and maybe they deserved each other," I interrupted him. "You're not telling me a thing I don't know already."

"I'm trying to tell you the way it was," he said sourly. "It was her idea they should take off and Rickie figured that was just fine—he knew all about her mother and all the dough in the family. Looked like a real good deal —he'd have his kicks with the broad and when he got tired of her, he'd do a deal with her old lady. Rickie figured she'd pay plenty to buy him off and avoid any scandal."

"He didn't know how Mrs. Summers felt about her daughter?" I said doubtfully. "All that refined hate?"

"Rickie found that out later," Ray said with a grimace. "He started remembering the Mann Act and the rest, and got real worried. They were running out of money fast, too, and when he mentioned it to the kid he got another

44

shock—she's not worth a dime until she turns twenty-one."

"That motel looked the right kind of place to get disenchanted," I said. "What else?"

"She told him not to worry about money—if things got real tough she could always get plenty. When he asked her where from, she just laughed and told him never to mind, the guy was loaded and she had him in a corner. After that she clammed up and wouldn't say any more about it. Rickie figured maybe she was just dreaming and came over here to see me."

"Looking for help from Big Brother," I said. "So you gave him advice instead of money, which is a hell of a lot cheaper—told him to marry the girl."

"I figured that was the best way out."

"You went with them to Nevada?"

"Sure. Rickie needed someone along to handle the detail—he's too much of a dreamer, out of touch, you know—a musician."

"Yeah," I said. "I can see he'd need a piano-player along."

"So that's the whole story, Lieutenant."

"You're sure?"

"I gave it to you straight, with nothing left out," he said coldly. "If you want, I can invent some fancy detail."

"I'll accept that without reservation," I told him, "which is more than I can say about the rest of your story."

I stood up and lit a cigarette before I started toward the door. Ray Willis got to his feet slowly, his face tense.

"What now, Lieutenant?" he asked harshly. "You call in that vice detail?"

"Check," I said. "Whatever made you think I wouldn't?"

"You lousy—"

"That credit card of mine carries its own responsibilities," I said easily. "If you start now, you got the chance to play piano for the last time in the Double Zero."

He came around the desk fast, mouthing obscenities in a kind of mechanical frenzy, his arms outstretched in front of him, the fingers hooking toward my throat. I let him get within reaching distance, then stiff-armed him with the heel of my hand hitting the bridge of his nose. He staggered backward and thudded against the desk.

"You're not looking at this the right way," I said reproachfully. "Now you don't have any more problems, like old man Denby!"

For a moment he just looked at me, the hate flaring in his eyes, then his right hand dived inside his coat and came out holding a gun. I got so nervous my reflexes popped and I'd jumped him before I knew it. I guess I was lucky—I'd never have made it if I'd stopped to think first. The side of my hand chopped down on his wrist and the gun slid from his fingers to the carpet.

I grabbed the lapels of his coat, pulling him close to me.

"Ray," I said with great restraint. "Don't ever do that again."

Then I backhanded him across the mouth, the way he'd hit Joe Diment, and he had the exact same reaction—rocking back on his heels with his eyes closed tight.

"You got a violent temper, Ray," I told him. "Watch it, why don't you, or you'll be smashing skulls with a hammer before you know it."

He opened his eyes slowly and stared at me while he moistened his split lower lip with his tongue.

"I'll get you, Wheeler," he said hoarsely, "if it's the last thing I ever do!"

"You're sick, Ray." I mimicked the pious voice he'd used about Mrs. Summers. "Sick up here." I tapped the side of my head with one finger. "I feel sorry for you—you need help."

·6·

I GOT BACK TO MY APARTMENT JUST AFTER ELEVEN AND put the flip side of the Peggy Lee record on the hi-fi machine, feeling her warm voice and immaculate sense of rhythm soothe my nerve ends while I made a drink.

The drink was about shot when the buzzer squawked suddenly, breaking up the mood I'd been working on with Peggy's help. I went to answer it, trying to convince myself that Ray Willis had been kidding with his "I'll get you, Wheeler, if it's the last thing I ever do" jazz. Still, and all, I felt better after I'd opened the door and saw my visitor couldn't be Willis because nobody could change their sex that fast—whoever heard of surgery while-U-wait?

There was a faintly embarrassed expression on Ilona Brent's pixie face as she stood there.

"I hope I didn't drag you out of bed, Al?" she asked hesitantly.

"I don't mind," I said gallantly. "If it'll make you feel better, I'll let you drag me right back."

"Could I talk to you for a few minutes?"

"Any time," I assured her. "Come right on in."

When we got into the living room, I helped her remove the arctic fox stole and the atmosphere rapidly turned tropical. She wore a backless black faille dress, supported by a narrow halter strap. I looked at the creamy-white perfection of her shoulders, then finger-traced the line of her spine down to the small of her back where there was dress again.

She shivered suddenly. "Don't do that!"

"How could I help it?" I asked brokenly. "You thrust your beautiful—and naked—spinal column right in front of my eyes with no warning, no red lights, no howling sirens. It would unnerve a doctor, never mind a cop!"

She turned to face me, a slight smile on her lips, and I got the second shock. The dress was partially frontless, as well as backless, cut low enough to reveal the beginnings of the sharp swell of her full breasts and the deep cleavage between.

"Talk about me unnerving *you*!" she said in a slightly breathless voice. "That all-seeing stare of yours makes me feel I wasted my time worrying about dressing at all."

"That's positive thinking," I said approvingly. "Tell me some more."

She sat down in the nearest armchair, crossing her legs with that delightfully intimate rustling sound you don't get to hear so much any more. I figure the percentage increase in lonelyhearts clubs is in direct ratio to the increased popularity of bermuda shorts. The only mystery left about a dame wearing bermuda shorts is why the hell she won't diet and take some of that weight off her thighs.

"I thought maybe we could have a cozy chat like we did before, Al," she said. "Kind of unofficial?"

"Have it any way you like, honey," I told her. "I'm just happy to sit here and watch."

"Will you please be serious for a moment?" she sighed. "You figure I'm joking?"

"I had a busy time tonight after we left the Sheriff's office," she said. "It worries me, so I have to tell somebody about it and I couldn't think of anyone else but you."

"Make a great song title," I said. "Why don't you dream up some lyrics while I make us a drink. What would you like?"

"A whisky sour," she said promptly. "Don't tell me this is a problem because I just know you grow your own lemons in California!"

"In an apartment?" I queried.

"Sure," she said confidently. "They grow out of the bedroom wallpaper."

48

"I couldn't think of anyone else but you," I said out loud, getting back to that song title. "You—with your mind on the ball—those legs maybe five feet tall—growing lemons out of the wall—"

She shuddered. "That is a lyric?"

"Well," I said defensively, "just the verse maybe—the introduction. You figure out a chorus, huh?"

I got the lemon juice from the delicatessen-bought plastic bottle in the ice box, like any other Californian, then made the whisky sour for Ilona, along with the same old Scotch on the rocks and a dash of soda for me.

When I got back into the living room, Ilona had a dedicated look on her face which in my experience of dames means one of two things: either she's going to take off her clothes—or else try and convert me to one of those screwball religions that grow out of the wallpaper along with the lemons on the West Coast.

I put the glass into her unresisting hand, then sat opposite her, cradling my own drink in both hands while I tried to figure an angle where I could see past the black faille curtain that descended two inches above her knees.

"I couldn't think of anyone else but you," she said dreamily, "to give all my subpoenas to—"

"It was strictly my mistake!" I said hurriedly. "Why don't we forget the whole deal?"

"You'll listen to my problems?" she asked in a kidding-on-the-square voice.

"Anything but more lyrics," I agreed.

"I had visitors around ten tonight," she said. "Angela and Rickie Willis—they came straight to the hotel after they left the Sheriff's office. Angela didn't waste any time coming straight to the point, she wanted to know if I'd represent them legally. I told her I could only do that if her mother agreed, so she said she'd go see her mother right away—leaving me alone with her intellectual playmate!" Ilona made an expressive face. "I don't even speak the same language as that moron!"

"It's basically English," I said. "Rickie's is just a little more basic than most people's."

"Anyway," Ilona continued, "a long half-hour later, Angela came back all excited, with a flushed face and an air of triumph. She waved a roll of bills at me and said it was a retainer, also I needn't worry about my fees, there was plenty more where that came from. I told her to keep the money and I'd talk it over with Lyn—her mother. Then she told Rickie they were now staying at the Starlight and didn't have to go back to the crummy hotel they'd been staying at up until then—she'd just gotten them a room two floors down where they could be nice and private."

"Everloving Mom sure pulled a switch," I said.

"That's what I thought," Ilona nodded. "So I went along to her suite and saw her. When I told her about Angela she looked at me like I was crazy and said she'd never even seen her, let alone given her any money. So that left me all confused and I'm still feeling the same way!"

"One of them has to be lying," I said cleverly.

"My instinctive choice would be Angela," she said. "But where would she get all that money except from Lyn?"

"How about Hillary?"

She shook her head slowly. "I can't see him giving her a wad like that because she just walked in and asked for it. And there's something else."

"Like what?"

"Like that marriage certificate," she said. "I had a good look at it after they'd gone. It's a fake—not even a good one."

"You're sure?"

Ilona looked at me icily. "Next question?"

"Yeah—sorry." I finished my drink and waited a couple of seconds while she emptied her glass. "So why the fake marriage—just to fool Momma?"

"I guess so," she said. "Like I said, Al, I was getting tired of being confused all by myself."

I made fresh drinks and when I got back to the living room, she'd gotten up from the chair and was looking at my hi-fi rig.

"You're a hi-fi buff?" she asked as I gave her the new drink.

"In a mild kind of way," I said. "Not real gone addiction—I still like hearing music better than the sound of termites eating through concrete and all that jazz."

"Play some music," she said softly.

I took Julie London's "Calendar Girl" album out of the rack and put it on the machine. Julie is the girl for late nights and low lights—and the fidelity of my five speakers match the fidelity of her voice.

"That's nice!" Ilona said a couple of minutes later.

"Very relaxed," I said. "You don't get to appreciate it fully, standing up. Why don't we relax on the couch and listen?"

"I know there's a good answer to that question someplace," she said thoughtfully. "Right now I just can't think of it."

She kind of drifted across the room to the couch and sat down and I heard that intoxicating whisper again as she crossed her legs. I sat down beside her, close but not too close because the night was young and I didn't want to turn it into an aging, sleepless night alone just because I got impetuous—that's a cute word meaning to grab with both hands.

"Do you think they did it, Al?" she asked suddenly. "I mean, with that fake marriage, how can we believe anything they say?"

I leaned my head against the back of the couch, missing her shoulder by a half-inch. "I'm relaxed," I said reprovingly, "and Julie's relaxed. What's with you, you got to be different?"

"Please!" she said tensely. "I have to know! Do you think Angela and Rickie killed that little man in the motel?"

"They're prime suspects," I said. "But there's no proof, not yet anyway."

"Proof or not, you must have made up your own mind, Al?" she persisted. "Do you *think* they did it?"

"How could I sit around thinking and be a cop at the same time?" I said. "Thinking is for intellectuals—the boys who figure out how to rig quiz shows and sell more sharkfin soup by making it a status symbol."

"My God!" she said hopelessly. "Now I get philosophy—the barefoot boy on the beat. Flat feet gave him a whole new outlook on life! He never knew what he was missing until he got a larger size pair of boots."

"It finally penetrated Angela's pointed little head that they are the two chief suspects," I said. "She was but intrigued to realize her mother, uncle, and their legal aid were in town the night Marvin was murdered. She said I should check on your alibis first and quit bothering her. What do you think?"

"I think she's a nasty little—" Ilona sighed deeply. "But thinking is out, I forgot. Alibis? I don't know—we got into the hotel and then the three of us had dinner around eight in Lyn's suite. Hillary left around nine-fifteen and went back to his own suite as far as I know. I stuck around talking with Lyn for maybe another quarter-hour then went back to my own suite and went to bed."

"Maybe that Angela has something," I said. "None of you have an alibi?"

"None of us have a motive either," she said easily. "Lyn hired a private detective to find her runaway daughter and Hillary recommended a man he knew. Why would either of them want to kill him once he'd done the job they'd paid him for?"

"Maybe he had a West Side address in New York?" I said hopefully. "And they couldn't bear the shame and humiliation of knowing him?"

"*I'll remember April*," Julie London's intimate voice whispered out of the five speakers.

Ilona lay her head against my shoulder and sighed deeply without saying anything.

"This Rickie Willis," I said. "Did you know he's an ex-con?"

"Well," she said dreamily, "what the hell?"

"I thought you were the one all worried and confused."

"I thought you were the one all relaxed," she countered. "Julie's relaxed—I'm all relaxed. Why do you have to get tensions now?"

"It's my sense of timing," I admitted. "It's been shot to hell ever since that night I knocked on the door of a blonde's apartment and as soon as it opened, said, 'Baby, love me tonight!'—then thrust a bunch of roses into the arms of her truck-jockey husband."

She gurgled with lazy laughter for a few moments. "Maybe you should put me on a permanent retainer basis, Al. You must need a lawyer nearly all the time."

Then her head turned toward me slowly, the hazel-flecked eyes molten and melting, her soft mouth open. I kissed her with the dynamite technique of the short fuse and long explosion, my arm sliding around her bare shoulder and my finger tracing the downward curve of her spine again. She shuddered, pressing herself harder against me, as her fingers dug cruelly into my chest.

A long time later she gently disengaged herself from my arms and stood up. Her midnight-colored hair made a tousled frame for the pixie face as she looked down at me for a moment.

"Too many lights in here," she said unsteadily. "You're nothing but a spendthrift, Wheeler."

She moved around the room, switching off the lights until the only illumination came from the shaded lamp on the corner bracket set above the hi-fi machine. As she walked back toward the couch, her fingers fumbled with the halter strap, and two seconds later the black faille dress slid down over her hips with a gentle rustling sound to her ankles. Underneath she wore a strapless black satin bra and half-slip, and her fingers were busily unfastening the bra as she stepped neatly out of the dress. By the time she got back to the couch she was naked except for the black satin panties which had generous inserts of fine lace.

The soft light gave a luminous sheen to the pearly-whiteness of her full, taut breasts as she leaned down toward me.

"I doubt if this is legal, but I'm sure there's a precedent," she whispered.

"This must be the avant-American look all the girls are wearing this season?" I said admiringly.

She grabbed two fistfuls of my shirt and hauled me to my feet. "I hate couches," she said simply. "They always give me a feeling of insecurity."

53

I put one arm around her shoulders and the other under her thighs, lifting her into my arms. She purred contentedly as I carried her toward the bedroom.

"That September," Julie sang intimately, *"in the rain."*

·7·

MR. JONES, THE MOTEL MANAGER, DIDN'T LOOK ANY BET-ter next morning when I saw him for the second time. His need for a shave had gotten twenty-four hours greater, the blue shirt a little more faded, the gray pants a couple of extra creases in the wrong places.

"You keep on coming out here for no good reason and I'll start charging you rent, Lieutenant," he said sourly.

"I want to take another look at both those cabins," I told him. "It's too early in the morning to argue and you look obscene in strong sunlight—so just give me the keys and I'll go look, huh?"

He grunted and spat at a nearby gray, trashcan-wise cat that dodged disdainfully, its fur bristling.

"O.K.," he grunted. "But make it fast will you, Lieutenant? Cops around the place are no good for my business."

I took the keys from his reluctant fingers. "It's you that's no good for your business," I said thoughtfully. "You look like an awful warning to any young guy about to embark on a night of vice. Why don't you get smart and get yourself a job with a temperance outfit playing a reformed alcoholic—you'd make a fortune!"

There was no percentage in waiting for his answer, so I didn't. I spent the next hour going over both the cabins again, inch by inch—I didn't have a fine-tooth comb with me because my teeth aren't the combing kind—but I did a real job on both cabins and came up with a double zero again to match the name of Ray Willis' key club.

Mr. Jones was in his office, his chair tilted back and both feet on the desk when I came in. I dropped the keys between his ankles.

"You find anything you couldn't find yesterday, Lieutenant?" he asked.

"Not a thing," I said. "It doesn't figure—not with Marvin, anyway. I never saw a guy travel so light—not even a spare shirt."

"He had a bag," Jones said. "Cheapskate beat-up suitcase—canvas kind."

"Why didn't you tell me that before?" I snarled. "Where is it?"

"You never asked me," Jones said, shrugging his thin shoulders. "I got it here—but there's nothing in it worth anything." He planted his feet back on the floor and leaned down behind his desk for a moment. He lifted a shabby mustard-colored bag and put it down in front of him. "Look for yourself," he said calmly.

Right then I was so mad I couldn't say a word—and for Wheeler, that's going some. I stared at him hard enough to curl him at the edges, and he didn't even blink.

I snapped open the clasps and lifted the lid of the suitcase. Dirty socks, underwear, shaving things. In the bottom a fresh shirt—or at least it had come from a laundry and was folded around a shirt board; it was badly frayed and gray at the collar.

"Sure there's nothing here you can use?" I said to Jones acidly as I tossed the contents one by one onto the desk. When I lifted the shirt, a large envelope that had been tucked inside it slid out. I saw Jones jump. "Guess you overlooked something, huh?"

It was addressed to Albert H. Marvin, at a West Side address in New York; at the top of the lefthand corner was the return address of the motel. It had not been through the mails, and it figured that it was something Marvin himself was mailing to his home address.

I slit it open with my thumbnail and shook out the contents. Seven or eight photographs fluttered down on the scarred wooden desktop, and when I shook the envelope a second time, a bunch of negatives followed.

"Hey!" Jones said hoarsely. His feet hit the floor with a crash as he craned his neck forward for a closer look. "Ain't they something!"

Look at them any way at all—and Jones sure did—they were something all right, with the same graphic intimacy of French postcards except the protagonists weren't anonymous. You could recognize Angela and Rickie in every one of them. I scooped up the pictures and negatives and put them back into the envelope.

"You don't have to be in such a hurry, Lieutenant!" Jones said plaintively. "I hardly got a good look at any of 'em. How about—"

"You're a dirty-minded old man," I said, stating an obvious truth. "Keep going this way and you'll never make one of the better-class cemeteries. No self-respecting embalmer would touch you even now, not even wearing rubber gloves!"

"What a dame!" he said coarsely. "What a figure! Hey, Lieutenant—you get a good look at her—"

"Have you got a camera?" I asked him suddenly.

"Why, sure." He scratched his head slowly. "But what—"

"We never found any camera in Marvin's room," I said in a hard voice. "With that fur-lined sewer of a mind you got, maybe you sneaked over to their cabin, nights, and took those pictures?"

"You're crazy!" he snarled. "I wouldn't—"

"That's it!" I snapped my fingers excitedly. "Sure—and Marvin caught you at it that night and scared the hell out of you so you killed him with the hammer, then dragged his body back to his own cabin. You got the pictures developed fast the next morning and you'd taken his bag so you could plant them in it and make it look like *his* dirty work."

"It was him!" Jones yelped. "That's his handwriting on the envelope! Look at his name in my register if you don't believe me!"

"You mean you wrote his signature in your book and the handwriting matches the writing here?" I asked coldly. "It all adds up—why else would you be fool enough to pinch that bag?"

He gibbered for a moment without being able to get any words out, then cleared his throat desperately and spat again, missing the open window by a minimum of two clear feet.

"I'll be back," I told him in my best "youdunit" voice as I pocketed the envelope. "Just don't try leaving town, huh, Jones?"

I drove back into town figuring I'd already done my good deed for the day—at least I'd given Jones something else to think about besides sex.

When I got back to the office, the ever-present Annabelle Jackson was present, wearing a shirt dress in charcoal-gray linen. It had sleeves that came right down to her wrists and should have given her a covered-up look, but didn't. The kind of figure Annabelle has would get through to you even in a Hawaiian muumuu.

"Hush ma mouth," I said admiringly. "You-all is pretty as a picture this morning, magnolia-blossom, honeychile, sweet memory of my ole Kentucky home."

"I'd love to hush that ole running-off mouth of yours —you aging Casanova," she said calmly. "With three beautiful women involved in this case, I wonder you have time to even see little ole me!"

"It comes from living a clean life, thinking clean thoughts, and cirrhosis of the liver," I explained. "My virility increases in direct proportion as my life expectancy decreases. Just one question before I go see the master?"

"No!" she said violently.

"Does your underwear whisper when you move?" I asked interestedly.

"You're disgusting!" Annabelle said, her face a sudden flaming red. "And it most definitely does not!"

"Aren't you worried you'll catch cold?" I said sympathetically, then ducked into the Sheriff's office before she threw something.

Lavers scowled at me as I closed the door and headed toward the nearest vacant chair.

"Where the hell have you been all morning?" he demanded.

"The motel," I said.

"Why waste your time out there when you're supposed to be catching a murderer?"

I figured maybe it was a good question because I couldn't figure out an answer, so I let it ride. Lavers rammed a cigar into his face and I watched, fascinated, while he lit it.

"How many cigars a day do you smoke, Sheriff?" I asked him.

"I don't know," he grunted. "Eight—nine. Why?"

"I bet you were a bottle-fed baby," I said. "The psychologists figure it shows a subconscious yearning for the warmth and safety found only at a mother's—"

"Wheeler!" He gobbled in fury for a moment. "Don't you ever get your mind off sex?"

"Sir!" I said reproachfully. "We were talking of your mother."

Lavers closed his eyes for a short while, giving me a chance to light a virile cigarette.

"All right," he said finally. "What did you find at the motel that's new?"

I took the envelope out of my pocket and pushed it across the desk toward him. While he goggled at the pictures, I gave him a run-down on the events since I'd left the office the night before. My visit to the Double Zero Club with Ray Willis—the facts that Ilona Brent had told me. The more I talked, the more I got the feeling he wasn't appreciating my efforts. When I'd run out of talk and just sat there, his beady eyes bored into mine with the ruthless speed of an electric drill.

"Of course," he said gently, "I'm only the county sheriff and I know I don't count for much around here. But I think you just might have had the courtesy to tell me what had happened before you sent the city vice detail into the Club!"

"You're so right, sir!" I said warmly. "And don't think for even one moment that I wouldn't have."

"Now you've lost me again!"

"If I'd sent the vice detail around to see Ray Willis, I'd have called you first, Sheriff," I explained.

His mouth sagged open and the cigar spilled out from between his teeth onto the desk. It was starting to burn a hole in his deskpad before he grabbed at it.

"You mean you didn't call them?"

"That's right, sir."

"He's running a bordello with a private key club as a front," Lavers said in a hushed voice. "He pulled a gun on you as well—but you didn't bother calling the vice detail." He looked at me almost apologetically, "I wouldn't want to embarass you, Wheeler, or anything like that, but under the circumstances I feel the question is necessary. Why didn't you call the vice detail about Willis?"

"I didn't want them fooling around with one of my murder suspects," I said truthfully. "You can't trust these city cops in a deal like that—first thing you know they'd have booked him or something stupid. I don't want Ray Willis slapped in a cell—I want him out in the open— for now, anyway."

"So he's free to commit another murder, if he is the murderer!" Lavers exploded. "And you're supposed to be a law enforcement officer. My God! I'm compounding the felony just sitting here listening to you!"

"Yes, sir," I agreed. "If it's any help, I'm working on those song and dance routines."

"What the hell?" he said hopelessly and relaxed back in his chair, taking cover behind a cloud of black smoke. "You think you have any kind of lead on the killer?"

"No leads, only complications," I said cheerfully. "That marriage certificate is a fake according to Ilona Brent—but I can't see that that means much more to us than discrediting the three of them—Angela and both Willis brothers. Or do we detect here the faint odor of red herring?"

"I don't have any answers," Lavers said. "Let's hear some more of your questions."

"Those pictures," I said. "Marvin must have used a camera to get them—he must have used his own developing equipment too. What happened to them? They weren't

59

in the cabin. They weren't in his suitcase—which, by the way, Sheriff, I left right where I found it. It can be picked up any time."

"Fine, Lieutenant," Lavers said with broad sarcasm. "And let me know when you trade in that form-fitting capsule of a car for something big enough to squeeze a suitcase into. It'll save the county a fortune in extra trips!"

"But why did he take the pictures anyway?" I went on, generously forgiving his insensitive attitude toward my Healey. "If it was for his client—Mrs. Summers—then why didn't he mail them to her, instead of himself?"

"Blackmail?"

"That's what it looks like, Sheriff," I agreed. "But who? Angela and Rickie?—Mrs. Summers?"

"I heard from New York this morning," Lavers said. "They check out Ray Willis' statement about his brother having a record. Rickie did two years for burglary, then a year on parole. He's clean now."

He sorted the papers in front of him. "They gave me a run-down on Marvin—he sounds like a real nice citizen."

"How's that?" I asked.

He lost his private detective's license six months back," Lavers said. "Mixed up in a call-girl racket—pandering at very high prices with maybe a little blackmail on the side. They didn't have enough to indict him, apparently, but enough to get the D.A.'s office to can his license."

"That's very interesting," I said. "For no good reason it makes me remember little Angela's suggestion we should look into the alibis of her family. Maybe Marvin was trying to blackmail Mrs. Summers—either directly, or through her brother-in-law. Could be the reason for planning to send the pictures to himself in New York—for safety."

"Could be," Lavers grunted. "Or maybe he was trying to lean on one—or both—of the Willis brothers? Either of them could have killed him with no trouble at all, by the look of their record."

"I guess I should go out and ask some more questions," I said. "You mind if I take those pictures with me? They might help get some answers."

"O.K.," Lavers said reluctantly. "But you'd better leave the negatives here."

I took the envelope, minus the negatives, and put it into my inside coat pocket.

"Before you go—answer me just one question," the Sheriff said grimly.

"The vice detail, sir?" I anticipated him. "I suggest we leave sleeping cops lie—to coin a brand new phrase."

"You sure you didn't make some kind of a deal with Ray Willis?" he asked suspiciously.

"Fifty per cent of a bordello?" I said dreamily. "It sounds like the wandering boy's dream of home, Sheriff. A regular unearned income every week and the freedom of the house. . . . Just call me Polly Wheeler! And I'd like you to know, sir, that any time you visit with us we'll gladly discount your tab fifteen per cent—for cash."

"Get out of here," he muttered morosely. "You're undermining my moral fibers!"

· 8 ·

"MISS ANGELA SUMMERS?" THE DESK CLERK AT THE Starlight said with a gleam in his watery eyes. "She's in six-seventeen—and Mr. Willis has six-eighteen, adjoining. Miss Summers insisted they have adjoining rooms. The maid tells me that six-eighteen is practically undisturbed."

"Gosh, Charlie!" I said admiringly. "You guys in the hotel business sure see life. I'll bet you've been to a burlesque show, even?"

"No need," Charlie said happily, "not after seeing

Miss Angela Summers. That Willis is a lucky guy—I'd sure trade my nights with him anytime."

"I wouldn't bet on it," I said. "You know if they're in?"

"Miss Summers is in—Mr. Willis is out," he said promptly. "Please remember, Lieutenant, the management frowns on attempted rape—it's a house rule."

"Then how come you're still working here?" I demanded. "No dame under forty-five ever gets past the desk without being deflowered by your X-ray eyes."

"It's a hobby, Lieutenant," he said smugly, "you know —like home movies?"

A couple of minutes later I knocked on the door of 617, and a muffled voice called out for me to come in. The door was shut but not locked, so I went inside the room and right away I figured that Charlie wasn't far out when he mentioned the house rule.

Angela Summers lay on the couch, her hands clasped behind her head, looking at the ceiling. She wore a gingham blouse in bronze check which was buttoned right up to the neck, giving her a demure look. The hem of the blouse came down as far as the tops of her thighs and underneath were a pair of white, fine silk-knit panties. Her long tanned legs were crossed at the ankles and her feet were bare, the toenails painted a mottled robin's-egg blue to match her fingernails.

She turned her head slowly and looked at me, the bird's-nest hair-do still the same inverted cone on top of her head. The big dark eyes looked at and through me with complete lack of interest.

"I figured it was Rickie," she said casually.

"I'll go outside again and wait till you get dressed, if you want?" I suggested.

"I'm dressed—aren't I?" She looked down at herself idly. "Sure—I'm wearing pants, so you don't need to take off!"

She swung her legs down off the couch, then stood up, stretching her arms above her head so that the pointed breasts thrust firmly against the thin blouse.

"I could use a drink," she said, and walked leisurely

across to the bureau and picked up the bottle that stood there.

"You want a drink, Lieutenant What's-your-name?"

"No, thanks," I told her. "And the name's Wheeler."

She poured bourbon into a glass and brought it back with her to the couch and sat down again, patting the empty space beside her.

"Why don't you take a load off your feet?" she asked in a bored voice. "You look like you're going to make with more questions."

I sat on the couch beside her, trying not to look at those beautifully sculptured legs the whole time.

"So make with the questions," she said. "Be my guest."

"Who faked the marriage certificate?" I asked gently.

"Who said it was faked?" she countered.

"You can take my word for it," I said. "Don't get cute."

She drank some of the bourbon slowly, watching me out of the corner of her eyes.

"Ray found out everloving Mom had arrived in town," she said finally. "We had to do *something*!"

"Why?"

"What's the matter with you—out to lunch?" she asked scornfully. "You know she wanted to pull that stat-rape caper. We figured she'd try and pull something like that—so we needed some kind of defense against her."

"Whose idea was the marriage certificate?"

"Ray's." She smiled, showing sparkling white teeth. "That Ray—he's the ginchiest, a real abominable snowman!"

"He's abominable, all right," I agreed.

"Don't be a drag!" she said coldly. "He's the nicest guy I know, next to Rickie."

"I hope you don't know Ray as well as you know his brother," I said.

"I'm not in orbit with that crack," she said with a question mark in her voice.

I took out the envelope and handed it to her. She pulled out the photos and looked through them with avid interest.

"Vavoom!" she said breathlessly. "And away we go!"

"They were found in Marvin's suitcase," I told her. "They just turned up today."

"He was a lousy grub!" she said. "Sneaking around the windows with his dirty little camera like this! Like there's no privacy even in your own pad any more!"

"Did you know he'd taken any pictures?"

"Of course not," she said. "What are you going to do with them, Lieutenant?"

"They're evidence," I said. "If you and Rickie had known about them, they'd have given you an excellent motive for murdering Marvin."

"We didn't know about them," she said hotly. "And we didn't murder Marvin. Why are you trying so damned hard to pin it on us, Lieutenant? Everloving Mom promise you a big fat bonus or something?"

"Yeah," I said nastily. "If I can hang the rap on you, I get to keep the pictures!"

She hauled off and slapped me across the mouth with the palm of her hand, and it hurt. The palm of my own hand itched until I had to do something about it, so I got to my feet and walked across to the bureau.

"I'll have that drink you offered me," I said. "Don't you have any Scotch around the place?"

"You're a kook!" she said wonderingly. "Why didn't you slap me right back?"

"Don't think I wasn't tempted," I told her. "I guess I'll have to settle for bourbon, seeing it's an emergency."

I made the drink and lit a cigarette to go with it.

"I'm—sorry," she said in a slightly hesitant voice. "I guess I asked for that crack."

"Marvin lost his license six months back," I said, watching her face in the bureau mirror. "He was mixed up in a call-girl racket—pandering, with a little blackmail on the side."

"You think he was going to try and blackmail us with these photos?" she asked.

"What good would it do him to blackmail you?" I said. "You don't have any money—or you didn't until last night."

"What do you mean?"

"You called on Ilona Brent," I said. "Left Rickie with her while you went to see your mother—you said. When you returned a half-hour later, you had what Ilona called a triumphant look on your face—and a fistful of money."

"Everloving Mom got soft and I made a touch," she said, then giggled suddenly.

"You never saw your mother," I said patiently. "She didn't even know you'd been inside the hotel."

"She was lying," Angela said without any conviction in her voice.

"You know she wasn't," I said, the patience bit wearing a little thin. "Anyway—we were talking of Marvin. Your mother hired him on your uncle's advice, did you know that? Hillary said he'd had dealings with Marvin before and he was a reliable operator."

"No," she whispered, "I didn't know that."

I sipped at the bourbon, then turned around to face her.

"The way things are now, Angela," I told her, "you might make eighteen O.K. but your chances of ever seeing nineteen are real lousy! Couple the circumstantial evidence with those pix as a motive and I could put you into court right now, with a seventy-thirty chance that a jury would find you guilty!"

She bit down on her lower lip until two pinpoints of blood showed. "But I didn't kill him!" she said dully.

"You made a couple of cracks about Hillary," I said idly.

"Something about him doing a lot of social work among the high school set? At the time I figured it was probably just one of your sweet girlish gags you throw at people all the time—but now I'm not so sure. I get curious about his relationship to the late Albie Marvin—was Marvin his panderer, maybe? I get curious why, after a half-hour alone with him last night, you come back with a flushed face and a wad of folding money. Maybe it's just the kind of mind I've got?"

"That's for sure!" she said quickly.

"Is it?" I looked at her for a few seconds, seeing the deep scarlet flush across her face slowly. "How many times do I have to say it, Angela? This is a murder rap you're facing. You're so close to it right now, you can reach out and touch it!"

"What do you want me to do?" she asked hoarsely.

"Tell me about Hillary," I said.

She drained her glass, then held it out toward me. "I need another drink."

I took the glass from her hand and went across to the bureau again, keeping my back turned toward her while I made the drink in slow time.

"I don't know about Marvin pandering for him," she said in a toneless voice. "I guess it could be. Hillary sure does have a thing about the high school set—I found that out before I went to Switzerland."

I took the fresh drink over to her, and sat at the far end of the couch. She lifted the glass to her mouth, tilted her head back, and drank the contents in one long gulp.

"He seduced me," she said casually. "Two months after my sixteenth birthday—a kind of late birthday present, maybe. I wasn't exactly innocent when it happened, but it was my first big deal. Do you have a cigarette, Lieutenant?"

I gave her the cigarette and lit it for her, and one for myself.

"It got to be a habit for a while," she went on. "I didn't really mind. Hillary is a gentle guy—and everloving Mom was crazy about him—had been even before Father died, I think. I guess I got a kick out of him choosing me for his bed instead of her. Then came the inevitable—she walked in on us one day unexpectedly. Maybe she'd gotten suspicious, I don't know, but she sure caught us at the right moment. You should have seen her! I thought she'd end up in a funny farm, the way she screamed and threw herself around. At one stage, she picked up an icepick from the bar and tried to cut his heart out with it! But that was it—vavoom!—Switzerland for little Angela!"

She drew hard on the cigarette, inhaling deeply. "So I guess dear old Hillary's always had a soft spot for me ever since that time. He's been useful—everloving Mom kept me on a tight allowance all the time, so when I needed cash I'd tell Hillary and he'd always come across with a respectable amount, like last night."

"A real nice guy!" I said with my teeth on edge. "Compared to him, Ray Willis is a gentleman!"

"Don't get mad at Hillary, Lieutenant"—she pouted her lower lip. "He's no different from any other man, after all!"

"I don't know too many forty-year-old guys who go around seducing sixteen-year-old girls," I said. "Do you?"

"They would if they had the chance," she said calmly. "You aren't forty yet—somewhere in your mid-thirties I'd bet, huh?"

"So I never made a pass at the high school set," I said. "Not since I left high school, anyway."

"How about a nearly-eighteen-year-old?" she asked in a soft, wicked voice. "If you had the opportunity?"

"Look," I said hastily. "Let's not—"

She laughed slowly—a harsh sound caught deep inside her throat. "What's the matter—chicken, Lieutenant?"

I watched as her fingers undid the buttons of her blouse, one by one, then came up on my feet with a nervous reflex. She stood up simultaneously, sliding her shoulders out of the blouse in a sensual movement, letting it slide down her back to the floor.

There was no bra underneath, so she was naked from the waist up. She took a deep breath which lifted her high, pointed breasts in a slow, lilting motion.

"Do I make you nervous, Lieutenant?" she said huskily. "I didn't mean to!"

She grabbed my right hand and cupped it around her left breast, squeezing my fingers hard.

"What's wrong, Lieutenant?" Her eyes searched my face for a moment. "You have some special kick, maybe? I'll put the blouse back on if you like and you can rip it off."

"What makes you think you're so special?" I said coldly, pulling my hand away. "I should be excited about taking candy from a kid—I'm not Hillary!"

A dull film shrouded her eyes as she still stared at me. "I should have known it was too late," she said venomously. "I guess everloving Mom beat me to the punch?"

The door opened suddenly and Rickie Willis came into the room. "Hey, Angie! I—" He stopped suddenly.

I saw the gleam in her eyes a fraction of a second before her hand exploded against the side of my face.

"Leave me alone, you dirty maniac!" she screamed hysterically. "Don't touch me!"

She ran into Rickie's arms, clinging to him fiercely with her head against his chest while she sobbed convulsively.

"Keep him away from me, lover!" she moaned. "Don't let him touch me again! He's a maniac—he tore off my clothes, and all the time he kept on telling me what he was going to do when he'd finished! I thought you'd never get back, lover!"

Rickie Willis stared at me, his face darkening rapidly.

"Cop!" he said thickly. "Dirty, stinking cop! They're all the same—the lousy—" He pushed Angela away from him violently so that she staggered and fell to the floor.

She rolled over on one elbow, watching me with a malevolent sparkle in her eyes. "Get him, Rick!" she whispered. "Get him good!"

He walked toward me slowly, his arms hanging down at his sides, the fingers clenching and unclenching spasmodically. To say he looked like a gorilla would be insulting evolution.

"I'll tear your guts out, you dirty, stinking cop!" he growled. "Laying your filthy paws on her, thinking just because you got a tin badge she's got to smile and say nothing about it!"

"You've got a lousy line of dialogue, Rickie," I told him. "Along with a limited vocabulary and a nonexistent brain. I don't want any part of her—she was trying me on for size. Maybe she wanted to keep in shape until you got back."

"Don't try and crawl out of it, copper!" he snarled. "You got it coming, man, and you're going to get it good!"

He was almost close enough to take a swing at me, and obviously in no mood for sweet reason. I was in no mood for a punch in the nose, either. I pulled the thirty-eight out from its belt holster and rammed the barrel hard into his navel.

"Take one punch at this dirty, stinking cop," I snarled at him, "and you'll get a dirty, stinking piece of lead right through your belly!"

He stopped right where he was and blinked at me a couple of times. "You wouldn't?" he said doubtfully. "Not with Angie as a witness."

"Try me?" I said softly, and rammed the gun an inch further into the softness of his stomach.

"He's only bluffing, Rickie!" Angela said shrilly. "Get him!"

Rickie licked his lips slowly. "He'd do it!" he said in a flat voice. "You can tell about this kind of deal—when a guy's kidding or he isn't." He turned his head and looked at her. "Sorry, honey, but there's nothing can be done—you dig?"

"You squirrel!" she said contemptuously. "You're chicken!"

"You must have some kind of a brain under all that hair, Rickie," I said. "Primeval as it may be. What was she wearing when you went out?"

"Huh?" He squinted at me blankly.

"Angela, you lamebrain," I said tersely. "What clothes was she wearing when you left?"

"A shirt," he said. His head turned slowly until he was looking at Angela, still sitting on the floor. He scratched his head, deliberating for a while. "And those white pants she's wearing now."

"I'm the guy who tore off all her clothes while you were gone," I explained carefully. "That means I ripped off her shirt—right? She's still wearing the pants!"

"Yeah," he said grudgingly.

I pointed at the blouse on the floor. "There it is, Rickie-boy. Take a good look. If there's one button missing you can hold the gun and belt me over the head with it."

"Don't listen to his lies, lover," Angela hissed. "He's just trying a snow-job."

Rickie stooped down and picked up the blouse carefully, then examined it with minute tenacity, checking off the buttons one by one. When he was finally satisfied, he tossed the blouse onto the couch, then walked stiff-legged over to the bureau, his hand reaching for the bourbon bottle.

Angela got quickly to her feet and ran across the room, throwing her arms around his chest and hugging herself against his back.

"You don't believe *him,* lover?" she asked softly.

He shrugged himself free of her enveloping arms, then turned around to face her, the drink in his hand.

"If I didn't know you better, baby," he said softly, "I'd figure you planned the whole deal so I'd stop a slug from the Lieutenant's gun."

"Rickie!" Her eyes dilated and she pressed the back of her hand against her mouth tightly. "You don't think I made it up?"

"Right now I'm not sure, baby," he said in an expressionless voice. "I got to think about it—figure it out, huh?"

He put the flat of his hand over her face in a casual gesture, then the thick fingers tightened into a hard painful grip as he pulled her toward him—like the start of a pitcher's windup—then pushed her away, letting go his grip on her face at the last moment when his arm was fully extended.

It was a miniature study in controlled violence. Angela almost flew across the room until her back hit the opposite wall with a sharp explosive sound. She crumpled onto the floor and lay there making faint whimpering sounds, her face gray as she tried desperately to get some air back into her lungs.

"Don't crowd me, doll," Rickie said mildly. "How can I figure it out when you're all over me the whole time?"

I started to walk toward her and Rickie grabbed my arm with a heavy, restraining hand.

"She'll be O.K., Lieutenant," he said. "She's a real tough baby under that delicate skin! And she had it coming."

"Whatever you say, Rickie," I agreed politely, turning toward him, showing him a man-to-man understanding of woman troubles on my face.

At the same time I pivoted up on the balls of my feet

and let him have my right fist just under the heart with all my weight behind it. I used that arm like a piston, giving him two more in quick succession, and by the time he got the third one he was wrapped around my arm like a pretzel. I cuffed his shoulder with the heel of my left hand so he toppled sideways and dropped onto the couch, out cold.

"And you had that coming, Rickie-boy," I said unnecessarily.

Angela had managed to get up on her hands and knees by the time I got to her. I put my arm around her shoulders and helped her shuffle across to the bathroom. Once we were inside, she shook her head violently and gestured mutely for me to get the hell out.

It was another emergency, so I had a little more of the bourbon, figuring if I hung around Angela Summers long enough, I'd develop a taste for it. Two, three minutes dragged by with Rickie still out cold on the couch, then Angela came back into the room, walking slowly, but looking a little better.

She opened a bureau drawer and took out a sweater and the black stretch nylon pants, pulling the sweater down over her head first, then stepping into the pants and wriggling them up over her hips.

"You know something, Lieutenant?" she said in a thin voice. "I spent a whole year in that Swiss finishing school and it was all wasted—they didn't even tell me how to take care of a situation like this!"

"Even Emily Post would need to think twice," I said politely. "You want me to stick around for when Rickie wakes up?"

"I think it would be better if you weren't here when he does," she said. "But thanks for the offer."

"Just one more question before I vavoom!" I said. "Where were you yesterday when you weren't in Nevada?"

"We went to Ray's club," she said tiredly. "We sat around and killed a bottle and cooked up the marriage-in-Nevada deal when Ray produced that phony certificate."

I walked to the door and opened it, then looked back at her. "You're sure you can handle him when he wakes up?"

"Sure." She nodded her head irritably. "I guess this is a big day in my life, Lieutenant. If I'm not getting a college education, at least I'll graduate from the school of H.K. Hard knocks, that is!"

"Sure," I said sympathetically, "and like Rickie said—you had it coming!"

· 9 ·

I KNOCKED ON THE DOOR OF THE SUITE TWO FLOORS UP, and a different world away, from 617. Hillary Summers opened the door and looked at me with an expression of mild surprise on his face.

"Lieutenant Wheeler, isn't it?" he asked pleasantly.

"That's right," I said. "I wanted to talk with you, Mr. Summers."

"Sure." He opened the door wider. "Come right in, won't you?"

We got settled in the living room, sitting opposite each other, with Hillary trying a little too hard to look perfectly relaxed.

"What can I do for you, Lieutenant?"

"You could tell me something about Marvin," I suggested.

"I don't think I can help much there." He shook his head regretfully. "I hardly knew the man."

"But you advised your sister-in-law to hire him?" I said.

"That's true," he nodded quickly. "I employed him to do a couple of small jobs for me and he was efficient, so naturally when Lyn talked of hiring a private detective to find Angela and the Willis boy, I suggested Marvin for the job. But I can't say I knew him at all, Lieutenant, not in the real sense of the word."

"Did you know he lost his license six months back?"

"No, I didn't!"

"He was mixed up in some call-girl racket—pandering with a little blackmail on the side," I added.

Hillary shrugged his shoulders awkwardly. "I had no idea. I would never have dreamed of recommending him to Lyn if I'd known."

I took my time about lighting a cigarette, watching his lean, sensitive fingers drum a soundless tattoo on his knee.

"Angela Summers came to see you last night?" I asked abruptly.

"Why do you ask?"

"She left Rickie Willis in Miss Brent's suite, then paid you a visit—although she told Miss Brent she was visiting with her mother."

He brushed the dark, gray-flecked hair back from his forehead with a curiously boyish gesture. "Well, yes, she did drop in and visit with me for a few minutes, Lieutenant. She wanted to leave the sordid hotel where she was staying and move in here—she asked me if I would make the arrangements for her, so I called the manager right away and fixed it."

"And gave her some money?"

"After all"—he smiled wanly—"she is my niece."

I took the envelope containing the photos out of my inside pocket and handed it to him.

"We found this among Marvin's things," I said.

He took the pictures out of the envelope and leafed through them slowly, staring at each one in turn.

"This is infamous!" he croaked, the blood draining from his face. "I'm surprised you haven't destroyed them already!"

"They're evidence, Mr. Summers," I said. "Maybe they provide a motive for Marvin's murder."

"You can't possibly think Angela had anything to do

73

with it?" he said hotly. "Maybe the Willis boy—but Angela!"

"I think anyone could have killed him," I said, "including you, Mr. Summers."

"What!"

"I understand from Miss Brent you both had dinner in Mrs. Geoffrey Summers' suite that night?"

"That's true."

"You left around nine-fifteen?"

"I know it was sometime after nine—why?"

"What did you do then?"

"I came back in here and went to bed."

"I don't suppose there's anyone who can substantiate your story?"

"I don't think that's amusing, Lieutenant!" he said in a bleak voice.

"So you don't have an alibi for the time of the murder?"

"Are you implying I need one?" he asked incredulously.

"Yeah," I said simply.

He got out of the chair and started to pace up and down the room, his hands thrust deep into the pockets of his beautifully cut Italian silk suit.

"This is ridiculous!" he said finally. "I have no intention of allowing you to walk all over me, Lieutenant. If you wish to continue this interview, I insist that Miss Brent be present, as my legal representative!"

"That's O.K. by me," I said. "You want her to hear Angela's story of your close relationship, I don't mind."

He stopped pacing suddenly and swung around toward me, a haggard look in his eyes.

"What do you mean?" he whispered.

"She just told me the whole story," I said flatly. "How you seduced her a couple of months after her sixteenth birthday—how her mother caught the two of you later and bundled her off to that school in Switzerland."

He sank back into the chair and buried his face in his hands. "She—she threw herself at me!" he muttered.

"It's bad enough the way it is now," I said contemptuously. "Don't make it worse!"

"I need a drink," he said thickly. "You'll excuse me."

74

He got up again and went over to the small bar set in one corner of the room and opened it up, displaying a half-dozen bottles.

"That's how you got to know Marvin in the first place?" I asked. "He was your panderer—around the high school set?"

"You can't prove that," he said dully.

"Maybe," I said. "I don't know yet—we can try."

He made himself a drink and gulped it down quickly, then replenished the glass right away.

"Why would Marvin bother taking those photos?" I went on. "There's only one logical reason and that's because he was going to use them for blackmail. But who was he going to blackmail, Mr. Summers? Not Angela or Rickie Willis—they didn't have any money. Not Angela's mother because she wouldn't have given a damn—in fact they could have helped her bring her charge of statutory rape against Rickie. That leaves just you!"

He swallowed most of the second drink quickly, then looked at me with savage, impotent hate in his eyes.

"You're out of your mind!" he snarled.

"And you have no alibi for the time Marvin was murdered," I said. "If you drove out to the motel or some other meeting-place to see him that night, there'll be somebody, someplace, who saw you—and I'll find them, Mr. Summers."

I got up out of the chair and walked toward the door. "And when I find them," I added. "I'll book you for first-degree murder and you'll wind up in the gas chamber."

"Get out!" he said thickly. "You hear me? Get out!"

"I was just going," I said reasonably. "If you get tired thinking about the gas chamber, Mr. Summers, you can always think about the sensation Angela's going to be in court when she gives evidence about her intimate relationship with you. You're going to be front page news on a world-wide basis then!"

I stepped out into the corridor, closing the door behind me gently just as the phone started to ring inside. I walked along the corridor to the next suite and knocked on the door, beginning to appreciate the problems of a traveling salesman.

A badly dyed blonde in a maid's uniform opened the door and looked at me haughtily, like I wasn't what she expected to be calling on a quarter-billion dollars.

"I'd like to see Mrs. Summers," I said.

"I'm sorry." She looked down her sharp nose at me. "Mrs. Summers is resting and doesn't wish to be disturbed."

"Don't we all?" I sighed regretfully. "I'm Lieutenant Wheeler—from the sheriff's office—I think she'll see me."

She glared at me for a moment, then said reluctantly, "I'll find out." The door closed in my face abruptly.

It looked like that was another vacuum cleaner I hadn't sold today. I checked my watch and saw it was just after five—it had been a long afternoon and that steak sandwich I'd had for lunch was only a memory. Then the door opened again and the maid was back, complete with glare.

"Mrs. Summers said for you to wait in the living room," she said shortly.

I followed her inside and she gestured with one finger toward a stiff-backed chair.

"You're kidding!" I told her cheerfully, and gave her a cosmopolitan, man-about-town, slap across the bottom as I walked past her toward the couch.

She squealed indignantly. "You—you *beast!*"

"How come you never married?" I asked interestedly as I settled down onto the couch.

Her curiosity fought a short, sharp battle with her outraged virginity, and won. "How did you know I wasn't married?" she asked sharply.

"One look," I said happily, "and it figures!"

She marched out of the room, her back stiff with frustrated fury, and I relaxed against the cushions of the couch. Maybe ten minutes later, Mrs. Geoffrey Summers came into the room.

She wore a negligee in a rich white satin, hand-embroidered, I guessed, in gold thread. The same tall, slim blonde—all elegance and fine steel—with icy-cold, deep blue eyes. I stood up as she came into the room, and she made a small, impatient gesture with one hand, telling me to sit down again.

"Is this visit of some importance, Lieutenant?" she asked crisply. "Or just a routine call?"

"I wouldn't say it was routine," I told her. "Did you bring the maid with you from the East Coast?"

She closed her eyes and shuddered delicately. "I wouldn't employ her to wash dishes at home! She's the best I could get from a local agency, and the best proof anyone could have that traveling in the less civilized areas of this country is something to be done only after adequate preparation, or preferably not at all!"

"I figure no nose could be that pointed unless it's been pressed against a million keyholes," I said.

Mrs. Summers straightened her already-straight back another half-inch. "Vera!"

"Yes, ma'am?" The maid came into the room, looking at her inquiringly.

"I won't need you any more today," Mrs. Summers said. "You can go now."

"Yes, ma'am," the maid said regretfully, and gave me a dirty look as she walked toward the door.

Mrs. Summers waited until the door had closed behind the maid, then sat down opposite me in an armchair, the white satin whispering richly as she crossed her legs.

"Now," she said briskly, "what do you have to tell me that's so confidential we can't risk the maid hearing it, Lieutenant? That you've arrested Rickie Willis, I hope?"

I went into the routine that was getting monotonous again, wondering if I should use a phony French accent to go along with the postcards. She took the envelope out of my hand, extracted the pictures, and looked at them with an icily remote expression on her face. Ten seconds later she handed them back to me.

"Well?" she asked calmly.

I told her how I'd come by the pictures, how I figured Marvin had intended to use them for blackmail.

"I don't see how, Lieutenant," she said. "Angela had no money at all to pay him—and I wouldn't have given him a penny for them."

"Not even to use as proof of statutory rape against Rickie Willis?" I prodded.

"There was plenty of other evidence," she snapped. "As I told you before in that grubby little office of yours. You have a short memory, Lieutenant!"

"One of my minor faults," I assured her. "I'm with you—he couldn't have blackmailed either Angela or you with them."

"So why did he bother?" she asked in a bored voice.

"Hillary might have paid big money for the negatives," I suggested.

"Hillary?" She raised her eyebrows fractionally. "What on earth for?"

"Angela told me the whole story an hour back," I said. "How he seduced her when she was sixteen years old—how you found out about it. Marvin lost his detective's license six months back because he was pandering for a call-girl service, suspected of blackmail, too. Chances are he was Hillary's panderer, too."

"Do you think all this intimate knowledge of yours makes you one of the family now, Lieutenant?" she asked in a dry, hard voice.

I tried to give an elegant shudder. "I wouldn't wish that on Rickie Willis, even!" I told her truthfully.

She made a hissing sound deep in her throat as she came out of the chair with her hand raised ready. I jumped to my feet and caught hold of her wrist, twisting it down, around behind her back so she was forced against me, hard enough for me to feel the soft curve of her breasts against my chest.

"You slap me, honey," I grinned at her bleakly, "and I'll slap you right back, quarter-billion dollars and all."

"Let go of me!" she panted, and tried to wrestle her arm free.

I never kissed that much money in my whole life before and I wasn't going to miss the opportunity now. I gave her wrist a gentle tug which forced her even harder against me, so I felt her fast heartbeat hammering against my chest. She reacted violently when our lips touched, jerking her head to one side. I grabbed the back of her neck with my free hand, making a clamp of my fingers so she couldn't move her head any more than an inch either way.

She froze then, letting me kiss her with a rising violence, standing immobile like a statue until I finally quit in despair, letting go of her wrist.

She looked at me stonily while she gently massaged her wrist. "I suppose I can't really blame you for thinking I'm no different from the rest of the family," she said in a strained voice.

"You're a very attractive woman, Mrs. Summers," I said sincerely. "Even if your emotional reactions are all deep-frozen."

I saw the sudden warmth come into her eyes and didn't believe it for a few seconds.

"Call me Lyn," she said suddenly. "It's ridiculous having a man who's just kissed you still saying 'Mrs. Summers.' You must have a Christian name—I refuse to say 'Lieutenant' any more. What is it?—something horribly small-town I imagine, like Elmer?"

"Al," I said wonderingly. "I guess it's no improvement?"

"Not much," she snapped. "Do you want a drink?"

"Always."

"There's some cognac in the kitchen—make mine over the rocks," she said briskly.

Mine not to reason why. I went out to the kitchen, found the cognac, and made the drinks. When I got back to the living room she was sitting on the couch waiting for me.

She took the glass from my hand and looked at me obliquely for a moment. "What do we drink to, Al? Your masculine virility, I suppose?"

"Coupled with your feminine curves," I said. "Or maybe I should put that some other way?"

"It'll do," she said, and sipped the cognac sparingly. "I imagine Angela was with Hillary last night when she was supposed to be with me?"

"That's right," I agreed. "Tell me something—why do you hate her so much? You must have worked at it for a hell of a long time."

She rocked her glass gently, watching the ice cubes

79

knock against the rim. "I was eighteen when I married Geoffrey," she said in a low voice. "By the time I was twenty, Angela had been born, and I was too old for him. He just wasn't interested in girls over nineteen, so from then until his death, I had to watch him getting older and his playmates getting younger each year. Oh, everyone thought our marriage was successful enough and there was one good reason for not divorcing him— Angela. I didn't want her name sullied by the exposure of her father's philanderings with high school and college girls!"

"If you hated him, it figures," I said. "But why hate Angela?"

"Because she's her father all over again," she said tautly. "I didn't want to believe it at first, I closed my eyes to it, pretended I was imagining the things that happened from the time she reached fourteen, on. When the principals of all those exclusive private schools tried to tell me—so discreetly—what was the trouble, I refused to believe them. Then came the episode with Hillary and I had to believe it!"

"Maybe that was more his fault than hers," I said tentatively.

Lyn shook her head determinedly. "I should have guessed that Hillary was cast in the same rotten mold as his brother—but I saw them, Al! If anyone had been seduced, it wasn't Angela. After that I sent her to school in Switzerland and she lasted there a year before they threw her out. When she came home I threatened and pleaded with her not to see Hillary—so inside six weeks she'd run away with that dreadful Rickie!"

She turned her head toward me and I saw the iceberg had finally melted, as the tears glittered in her eyes.

"I don't *hate* her!" she whispered hopelessly. "She's my child, how could I ever hate her? But when she ran away I thought I had only one hope left—to frighten her so much, she'd reform. That's why I talked statutory rape and the rest of it. I would never have gone through with it, Al, you have to believe that!"

"The night Marvin was murdered," I said. "The three

80

of you—Ilona Brent, Hillary, and yourself—had dinner in here?"

"Yes," she nodded.

"Hillary left first, around nine-fifteen?"

"It would have been around that time, anyway," she said.

"And you didn't see him again until next morning? He went back to his own suite, to go to bed?"

"Yes, but I saw him again, about twenty minutes later. I needed something to make me sleep and I'd run out of tranquilizers, so I went and asked him for some."

"He was there all right?" I asked gloomily.

"Of course. He gave me some pills and I came back here."

"That was all that happened?"

"I don't remember anything else."

"Was he in his pajamas?"

"No, he was still dressed. I wasn't in there more than five minutes and most of that time I was waiting until he'd finished with his phone call."

"What phone call?" I yelped.

"It rang just after I got into his suite," she said casually. "He spent about three minutes talking to whoever it was, while I waited."

"He didn't say who it was?"

"No, I think he was annoyed I was there—he was very guarded about what he said, just grunted most of the time."

"Can you remember any part of the conversation, other than the grunts?" I asked her hopefully. "Anything at all —it doesn't matter how disjointed?"

"Well—" she thought about it for a moment. "The only coherent thing I remember him saying was, 'Eleven o'clock—I'll be there,' or something like that."

"Nothing else?"

"I'm sorry," she smiled faintly. "Nothing else, Al. Does it help at all?"

"Could have been Marvin calling, and Hillary made a date to see him," I said. "But you couldn't offer it as evidence in a courtroom."

"You really think it was Hillary who killed him, and not that dreadful Willis boy?"

"Hillary had plenty of motive," I said. "Willis hasn't."

She finished her drink and offered me the empty glass. "What's the time, Al?" she asked indifferently.

"Five of six." I took the glass out of her hand.

"Don't they blow a siren or something when it's time for you to finish work?"

"Didn't you hear it?" I said. "The whistle just blew."

"I'm glad you heard it, anyway," she murmured. "I was beginning to wonder."

"I'll go make fresh drinks," I said brightly. "Even if I am disenchanted with the glasses."

"What's wrong with them?"

"I expected solid gold goblets, no less!"

"They might be all right for the Miami crowd, darling," she said with a grin. "But in my set they'd be considered ostentatious."

I went into the kitchen again and made the fresh drinks, then took them back with me to the living room. The night looked like it had fallen with a sudden thump —the room was nearly dark. When I'd left a minute before, the sun had been shining through the windows. It was no trick really to use my deductive powers and realize the room was near-dark because the shades had been pulled down and the drapes drawn across the windows.

Lyn Summers had vanished from the couch and while my eyes were still getting used to the near-dark, I couldn't see where the hell she'd gone. I parked the drinks carefully on a sidetable and went to sit on the couch again, then didn't. It wouldn't have felt right to crush all that beautiful satin and hand-embroidered gold thread. The adrenalin started to pump through my veins as I stood there looking at Lyn's negligee, getting a sharp mental image of how she must look without it.

There was a soft click, and a table lamp on the other side of the room glowed suddenly with a warm, diffused light. Lyn stood beside it, looking at me with an almost anxious expression on her face.

"You did say you heard the whistle blow, Al?" she asked nervously.

"Like a clarion call!" I said.

She came toward me slowly, the lamplight making intricate, everchanging patterns on her moving flanks, displaying her durable body in loving detail; the small, pink-tipped breasts that would never sag, the soft swell of her hips merging into the rounded firmness of her thighs. I took her into my arms when she got close and felt her body tremble slightly as it pressed against mine.

"You're scared?" I said softly.

"I'm thirty-eight years old," she said in a small, bewildered voice, "and right now I'm more nervous than I was twenty years ago, on my wedding night!"

"Hey!" I nibbled her ear lobe gently. "What's with this mixing sex and sentiment—a new kick?"

Her body relaxed suddenly as she laughed in a throaty gurgling sound. "I guess sentiment's considered ostentatious in the cops and robbers set," she said.

I ran my hands down the smooth back, following the indented curve of her waist, over the lithe, eager firmness of her flanks, and she stopped laughing in one sharp intake of breath.

It was a little after eight when I walked across the hotel lobby up to the desk, with the keen eyes of Charlie, the desk clerk, watching me the whole time.

"You been here so long, we should charge you rent!" he said. "Been on a high society kick, Lieutenant?"

I shook my head. "It's the drains again, Charlie. I've checked all over the hotel—but the real bad smell is coming from behind this desk. How do you figure that?"

Charlie's eyes gleamed as he looked me up and down carefully, then shuddered.

"I don't want to get personal, Lieutenant—but that suit! One of the County Sheriff's cast-offs, maybe?"

"Well, sure it is," I said defensively. "But I had it taken in a couple of feet around the waist already."

"I'm glad to hear it did belong to the Sheriff one time," he said happily. "When I first saw it, I figured you were on relief!"

He turned away to welcome a new guest—a tycoon-executive type with a bristling white mustache and blood-shot eyes.

"Good evening, sir," Charlie said deferentially. "Welcome to the Starlight Hotel!"

"Just one more thing!" I said loudly. "You tell the manager from me if he doesn't get that ceiling fixed tomorrow, I'm checking out. Took me a half-hour with a scrubbing-brush to get that stuff off my face this morning."

The tycoon-executive looked at me curiously. "Plaster?" he asked gruffly.

"Plaster, I wouldn't mind," I said bitterly. "Blood! The guy on the next floor up blew his brains out last night and that damned ceiling was still leaking at nine this morning."

"Suicide?" His eyes bulged alarmingly, and the bristle went out of his mustache in one *poof*.

"I guess you couldn't blame the poor guy," I said. "Had a busted leg and couldn't move out of his room. After two weeks eating nothing else but the hotel food, I figure blowing your brains out would be a ball!"

I turned and walked away from the desk quickly, but not quick enough to avoid hearing Charlie's soothing voice.

"He tries to be funny, sir," he said, pitching his voice loud enough to make sure I couldn't dodge it. "Used to be a professional comedian once, but he hasn't worked since they stopped making silent movies. I expect you noted the professional touches—the coat four sizes too big and the baggy pants? We try and help out where we can—he's just finished a job cleaning out the trashcans. I guess that's why he's so excited."

I revolved through the revolving door out onto the sidewalk, figuring I must be losing my grip—Charlie was always getting the last fifty words lately. The Healey was parked way down the street, and I started to walk toward it slowly, lighting a cigarette as I went. There was another interesting problem—did I smoke virile cigarettes because I was virile—or did smoking virile cigarettes make me virile? Either way I was just lucky, I guessed.

The sound hit my eardrums with almost physical force

—a thin wailing scream of absolute terror. I came to a sudden stop wondering for a split second where the hell it had come from. Then the snooty-looking redhead in a white mink jacket walking in front of me let out a wild yell and pointed upward.

I jerked my head back and saw what looked like a great white bird, with flailing wings, hurtling down out of the sky toward me. It increased in size with fantastic rapidity, then hit the sidewalk six feet from the redhead, with a horrible splitting noise, like someone had dropped an overripe orange.

I went past the redhead who was still screaming her lungs out, and saw the nude body of a man spread-eagled on its back across the sidewalk. An even wilder scream from the redhead made my head jerk around to see what was wrong. She stared at me blankly through glazed eyes, gesturing frantically at herself.

Then she took a second look at the dark, glistening wet stains splashed across the front of her jacket, befouling the white mink. Her knees gave way suddenly and she fainted on the sidewalk.

I got one quick look at the naked body pulped against the concrete before I went back to do something for the redhead. Just one quick look, but it was enough to see that the fear-distorted face, with its wide-open mouth and staring eyes, was recognizable.

It belonged to Hillary Summers.

· 10 ·

THE THREE OF US STOOD GROUPED AROUND THE BEDROOM window, looking down onto the sidewalk where Summers' body had landed thirty minutes before.

"Eight floors," Lavers grunted. "It sure is a hell of a

long way down. I never know how they get the nerve to jump—it's the worst way to do it!"

"Maybe he didn't jump," I said.

"You mean, Lieutenant," Sergeant Polnik said eagerly, "like—maybe he tripped?"

"Well," I rode herd on my baser instincts, "he was an athletic character, at that!"

"Most of the time, Wheeler," Lavers said heavily, "you appall me, but I can understand you only too well!"

"Thank you, sir," I said enthusiastically. "Do you wish to split the fees with my analyst?"

"But this one time I don't figure you out at all!" he growled. "You spend all day working up a case against Hillary Summers—you do your damnedest to frighten all hell out of him with it—to scare him into making a mistake. This, by your own mouth, as you told it ten minutes back. Right?"

"Right," I agreed.

"So he goes and makes the mistake," Lavers roared. "You scared him even better than you knew. You scared him so much he figured he had three strikes against him already—so he jumped out the window. You've proved your case and it's finished—you've done a good, fast job on something that could've turned real nasty if we hadn't gotten a fast result. Fine! Even I'll admit it was a nice piece of work. So then what do you do? You start yakking about maybe he was pushed—that we've got another murder yet!"

"It's just a feeling I've got," I mumbled.

"An inspirational cop!" he howled despairingly. "Did you bring your violin along—or are you using the ouija board this time?"

"I didn't know this guy too well," I said. "But maybe I got an insight this afternoon when he was bleeding there for a while. You saw him, Sheriff. A guy who's a multi-millionaire—a lean, sensitive character who had a big guilty secret to hide from everyone else. He was an odd-ball with young girls making his kicks—so in every other way he'd make himself look as normal as he could."

"Psychology yet!" Lavers snarled.

"It figures," I said patiently. "Summers wore nice, conservative and expensive, suits—the kind you'd expect a guy in his position to wear. I'll bet he never got drunk, picked up a ticket for speeding, shouted at waiters, complained about room service. . . . He was always trying to hide behind a mask of respectability, hoping people would take him at face value the whole time—because this was the only way he could keep his nasty little secret. He had, for sweet Sigmund Freud's sake!—a guilt complex. If Hillary Summers was going to suicide, he'd have done it in a quiet, gentlemanly way, like maybe cutting his wrists in a hot bath. But even if he got around to jumping out the window, he wouldn't have jumped *naked* —it would've been like admitting he chased teen-age girls into bed!"

"Why don't you take your brain someplace and get it washed?" the Sheriff asked disgustedly. "By me, the case is closed—Summers murdered Marvin—and that's the way it'll be unless you can prove different."

"All right," I said, breathing heavily. "So why don't you take your blood pressure out of here and let me get started?"

Lavers glowered at me for a few seconds, then rammed a cigar into his face with brutal disregard for his front teeth.

"All right!"—he bit off the words along with the end of the cigar. "I'll give you twenty-four hours, Wheeler, to come up with some proof that he was murdered. But not a minute more."

"Thank you," I said coldly.

"Be my guest," he said sourly, then stamped out of the bedroom. A few seconds later I heard the front door of the suite slam behind him.

Polnik looked at me wistfully. "Some case, huh, Lieutenant? All those gorgeous society dames mixed up in it. I bet you had yourself a ball—I, uh, guess there just ain't room for a sergeant?"

"Polnik," I said sadly. "I haven't treated you right in this case, have I?"

"Cheez!" he said emotionally. "You don't have to worry about me, Lieutenant. Maybe I'll get lucky next time around—but I sure would've liked to get close to the brunette again. You know, Lieutenant, the one who wears those black stockings right up to her waist?"

"Angela Summers," I said. "And they're stretch-nylon tights."

"If they stretch real good maybe I can get a pair to fit my old lady?" Polnik said thoughtfully. "Like maybe she'd look different?"

"Vavoom!" I agreed enthusiastically.

"My throat gets me the same way sometimes," he said. "You want a cough drop, Lieutenant?"

"I want you to catch up on what you've been missing, Sergeant," I said briskly. "Get into that diamond-studded, satin lingerie-d world you've been missing out on!"

"Cheez!" Polnik nearly choked with emotion. "You figure maybe I'll get to rub shoulders with them minks and chihuahuas and all?"

"Sure," I said. "Just watch it you don't get bitten."

"What do I do?" he asked happily.

"Check on Angela Summers and Rickie Willis first," I said slowly, giving each word time to penetrate the rocklike skull. "I want to know where they were when Hillary went out the window. I was on the sidewalk when he came down and it was eight-ten exactly."

"Got it!" Polnik snapped.

"Then check on Ilona Brent and find out where she was," I told him. "I'll take care of Mrs. Summers myself."

"O.K., Lieutenant. Anything else?"

"That'll keep you busy, Sergeant," I assured him. "I'll check with you in the office tomorrow morning around nine."

"You, Lieutenant?" he stared at me with his mouth open. "Inside the office at nine in the morning?"

"I didn't say I'd be there," I said pointedly. "I expect you to be there, so I can check with you. Maybe I'll use one of the newer things like this kid inventor, Alexander Graham Bell, has just come up with."

"Some kind of code, huh?" Polnik looked worried. "I sure hope you can make it easy, Lieutenant—they tossed me out of the vice detail because the numbers racket got me kind of confused once the numbers came into doubles."

"I'll make it simple," I told him. "Hadn't you better get started? Champagne in a sterling silver slipper goes flat awful fast!"

"I'm gone already!" he said gleefully, and he was.

I took a last look around the bedroom before I left the suite. Hillary's clothes were in an untidy heap on a chair, and that didn't figure. He'd been a neat character and habit doesn't die any quicker than its owner. It was the third argument against suicide, along with him being naked, and the sound of his scream as he came down. I guessed a guy might change his mind too late, after he'd jumped, but the way I heard it, it sounded like he was screaming from the first moment he started to fall.

I went out of his suite, along to Lyn Summers' door, and tapped on it gently. The door opened maybe six inches, then she saw who it was and it opened wider.

"Come on in, Al," she said. "I was just getting dressed."

After I got inside the living room and closed the front door behind me, I looked at her and saw she wasn't kidding. She wore a cream-colored bra made of heavy silk lace, and a pair of white, fine silk-knit panties, which made me wonder how often Angela had raided her mother's wardrobe.

"Come and talk to me in the bedroom so I can finish dressing," she said briefly, and led the way.

I leaned against the bureau watching, as she sat on the bed and pulled on a pair of nylons.

"You were obviously right about Hillary," she said coolly.

"Were you in here when it happened?"

"Yes," she nodded. "I was lying on the bed—" her mouth quirked at the corners momentarily "—resting!"

"Did you hear anything?"

"Nothing," she said flatly. "I wish I had—I might have been able to stop him."

She stood up and dropped the heavy satin slip over her head, smoothing it down over her hips until it sat smoothly, the bosom a froth of fine lace. Her eyes met

89

mine for a moment, and that ice-cold impersonal look came back into them.

"Please stop leering at me!" she said sharply. "There's nothing I detest more than that lecherous, old goat look!"

"Can I help it?" I said mildly. "That beautiful figure of yours, and all that satin and lace and silk jazz, doing a tease job at the same time."

"You might remember that tired old joke, Lieutenant," she snapped. "The punch line goes something like, 'Sleeping together is no valid reason for social introduction.' It sums up exactly the way I feel!"

"It's your privilege," I said. "Where are you going?"

"I don't know—anywhere," she said tautly. "I think I'll go mad if I stay cooped up in here any longer—after poor Hillary killing himself! I'm going out somewhere where I can find bright lights and soft music and lots and lots of people."

"So long as they're the right kind of people?"

"Where would I find them on the West Coast?" she said derisively. "Marineland?"

"You want an escort?"

"I'll put it into words of one syllable for you," she said in a murderously sweet voice. "Once in maybe every two years, when I'm suffering some deep emotional stress, I have a sudden, overwhelming need for a man—any man—the nearest man! Then I'm cured for the next twelve months at least. This afternoon, you were that man, Lieutenant. Is that clear?"

"Like glass," I agreed. "Just before I go sob my heart out in the nearest bar—tell me something I forgot to ask you before."

She opened the closet door and lifted out a short evening gown, pale blue chiffon. It looked a simple little number.

"This isn't the question," I said. "But I'm strictly a rubberneck—how much did you pay for that?"

"This?" She slid the gown off its hanger and stepped into it easily. "I spend an average of sixty thousand a year on clothes," she said calmly. "It's hard to remember the individual price tags, Lieutenant, unless it's something like a floor-length mink for the opera. That's special."

"You got me hooked," I admitted. "How special?"

"The last one cost me twenty-eight thousand," she said. "I wish you'd stop being such an inverted snob—it's faintly nauseating!"

"I'll stop," I said politely. "I should be grateful."

"How's that?" She raised the elegant eyebrows a premeditated millimeter.

"You might remember that tired old adage, Mrs. Summers," I said brightly. " 'A bitch in time saves nine'?"

"Most amusing!" she said thinly. "You can zip me up at the back before I go."

She turned her back toward me and I closed the zipper obediently.

"That question—I'd nearly forgotten," I said. "Did you pay Marvin, or did Hillary handle it?"

"I gave the thousand-dollar retainer to Hillary in the first place, to give to Marvin," she said.

"Was that the only payment made?"

"When he called me in New York to say he'd found them at the motel, he asked if I'd wire him another two thousand."

She slid her feet into evening shoes, then sat in front of the mirror, making last-minute adjustments to her hair and make-up. Then she fastened a sapphire and diamond pendant around her neck, and clipped on matching earrings.

"You sent him the money?" I asked.

"Of course. I was very pleased with his work in finding them so quickly. I wired him the money immediately—he would have gotten it in a few hours."

She stood up, draping a rich mink stole around her shoulders, then picked up her purse and walked toward the door.

"You could be useful, Lieutenant," she said as she reached the door. "You can ride down with me and call a cab."

"Don't be a piker, Lyn!" I said reproachfully. "Buy one, and have it sent up!"

The door slammed behind her, shifting the hotel's foundations a couple of feet. I waited maybe a minute, then left the suite. She wasn't anywhere in sight by the time I reached the lobby so maybe she had bought that cab.

I took the Healey from the curb and drove downtown at a pedestrian speed—I knew it was exactly that speed because a guy out walking his dog stayed level with me for three blocks. Maybe a half-hour later I parked outside the Double Zero Club. I was halfway across the sidewalk when I remembered it was a key club and the one thing I didn't have was a key.

While I was standing there wondering if anyone would open the door if I knocked, a guy walked past me and stuck a key into the door, solving all my problems. When he stepped into the small foyer I was right behind him, closer than a brother.

The stunning long-legged blonde in the black sequined bra and tights materialized from nowhere again, and took the guy's hat, then ushered him through the drapes into the main room.

"Can I take your hat, sir?" She smiled warmly at me, now it was my turn.

"Gee, thanks," I said earnestly. "Can I check my badge and handcuffs, too?"

Her smile faded fast as a look of recognition showed in her disturbingly brilliant eyes.

"Oh," she said flatly. "It's you again—the cop!"

"Wheeler," I smiled encouragingly at her. "Lieutenant Al Wheeler."

"How nice for you!"

"What's your name?" I persisted.

"Jerrie Cushman."

"Mr. Willis in his office?"

"I think so," she said. "I'll find out for you."

"I'll do it, thanks all the same," I said, and gave her my hat. "Take good care of it, honey. They don't make hats like that one any more."

She turned it over in her hands fastidiously. "Not since the Alamo," she agreed in a shaken voice.

"If you need any help finding another job, look me up,"
I told her. "I'm in the phone book."

"I already have a job, thank you!" she said coldly.

Then her head started to shake slowly, in time with
mine.

"I don't?" she said sadly.

"I got a feeling the place will be under new management soon, Jerrie," I said. "But—that's show biz!"

"But you wouldn't call it exactly legit?" She nodded
gloomily.

I walked past her, and as she held the drapes open for
me, she rubbed the back of her hand against the side of
my face gently, and I could almost hear the static elec-
tricity leap into sudden life.

"In the book, you said?" Her voice was a husky, intimate whisper. "I'll have to remember you, Al."

"I'll remember you, honey," I said truthfully, taking a
last look at her sequined bra and tights. "You're the girl
with the most poured into the least."

·11·

THE MAIN ROOM DIDN'T LOOK ANY DIFFERENT, AND THE
cigarette girl in the white bra and tights still gave me that
virile feeling as I walked past. I didn't bother to knock
on the door beside the timbered staircase; I just turned
the knob and went right on in.

Ray Willis and the beefy guy with all the brains, Joe
Diment, were inside the office having a drink. They both
looked up as I walked in, and from the expressions on
their faces I was welcome like the boll weevil in Annabelle
Jackson's home town. They both had one thing in com-
mon—a split lower lip.

"Hello, Lieutenant," Diment said unhappily and tried

to smile, then winced painfully as his lower lip refused to stretch.

"What's with you, Wheeler?" Ray Willis said nastily. "Couldn't you sell your story to the vice squad? Or did you chicken out on your double-cross after all?"

"I tell you this more in sorrow than in anger, Ray," I said in a melancholy voice. "I was in no hurry to get the joint closed down—not till I learned you'd let me down. You said you were telling the truth and I believed you. It hurts, Ray"—I put my hand over my heart—"right here. But now I got to do it."

"What are you talking about, Lieutenant?" Diment asked, with three chins quivering on the answer.

"Ask the boss. He knows," I said.

"Hey, boss—" Diment began, but Willis cut him off.

"Don't just stand there, you fat slob!" he snarled. "Get the hell out of here—this is no damned business of yours!"

"Sure, I'm going," Diment said unhappily. "How come things change so fast around here? Two minutes back we're having a social drink like we're buddies." By that time he'd reached the door, and he looked over his shoulder at Willis. "Now I'm a big fat slob again! It's getting like I don't even know who I am any more!"

"Get out!" Ray bared his teeth. "Before I split your top lip so they both match up!"

Diment leaped out of the office, pulling the door shut behind him.

Ray Willis looked at me and made a supreme effort, pulling a mask of contrite apology across his face.

"I heard about the Summers guy tonight, Lieutenant," he said. "Believe me it makes a difference to know the case is sewn up—now I can talk freely."

"No cover charge, Ray?" I queried. "Is that good for business?"

He smiled weakly. "I admit I lied last night about going to Nevada and those two kids getting married. It was just a gag in the beginning, and then it seemed like a good idea to stick with it when we heard about the murder and about Angela's mother's ideas about statutory rape and all that. You know how it is, Lieutenant—once it got started, I didn't have any choice. I had to go along with it, for the kid!"

"Your kid brother, Rickie?" I checked.

"Who else?" He lowered his voice a fraction. "He's the only folks I've got."

"Who wouldn't quit after scoring two like you and Rickie?" I agreed.

"I admit it was a stupid idea," he went on, shaking his head ruefully. "I guess I knew that certificate wouldn't fool anyone for long—hell, it was just one of a bunch of them I had made up once for a party—you know, to give the boys a morning-after shock—" He looked like he was going to wink at me, but I wasn't having any, so he got solemn again. "I just hoped it would make the cops pause a little before they nailed a murder rap on a couple of innocent kids who incidentally had a tie-up with Marvin. After all, a boy and girl in love and about to get married don't go around knocking off guys. But they were in a jam, and Rickie was scared stupid, and if you could've seen the way the kid had his arm around Angela, like to protect her, and all the time counting on me, his big brother, to get him out of the mess. Well, I tell you, Lieutenant, it kind of churned me up inside!"

"It churns me up inside too, Ray," I said sincerely. "I may vomit at any time now."

"I guess if I hadn't been way out on that emotional limb," he went on doggedly, "I would've told you right away last night that the certificate was a fake." He shrugged his shoulders resignedly. "But there it is, Lieutenant. The ball's in your court. You still want to close me up, it's your privilege."

"That's very generous of you to admit it, Ray," I told him.

He lit a cigarette, his fingers fumbling with the lighter for a couple of seconds, while his eyes looked every way but at me while he waited for my reaction.

I let him wait.

Finally he couldn't stand it any longer. "You see, Lieutenant, I knew Rickie and Angie hadn't killed anyone, but I had to do all I could to keep things slowed down a little till a smart cop picked the guy who really did it," he said. "And you did, Lieutenant!"

"It was nothing, Ray," I said modestly. "I just waited till Summers leaned out the window, then gave him a shove!"

He smiled uncertainly, "You sure got a strong sense of humor, Lieutenant!" Then he took a deep breath. "Well, what do you say? Do you close me up or are you giving me a break and just forget it?"

I picked up the phone on his desk and dialed Police Headquarters.

"Give me Lieutenant Johnson, vice detail," I said when a voice answered.

"What?" Ray came out of his chair slowly, a look of complete disbelief on his face.

I smiled at him while I waited for Johnson to come on the line. Ray's face underwent a startling number of different expressions in a very short time, like he'd just graduated from the Actors' Studio and was trying for an Oscar his first time out as a pro.

"You can't do this to me!" he said thickly. "You dirty, stinking, lousy cop!"

"I can tell you and Rickie are real close," I said. "You even talk the same way."

"I'm not letting you get away with it, Wheeler!" he bellowed suddenly. "I said before I'd get you if it was the last thing I ever did and—"

"Ah, shut up!" I told him. "I get sick in the stomach every time I listen to you run off at the mouth, Willis. The last time I was here, you pulled a gun on me, and I haven't forgotten that. The next time you even raise your voice a half-tone, I'm going to smear you around the walls!"

He stood with mouth wide open, gaping at me for a moment, then he pushed past the desk, heading toward the door in a blind, stumbling trot. Maybe he'd left his guts outside and had gone to get them.

"Johnson," a crisp voice said in my ear.

"I thought you were dead," I said conversationally. "But you were just giving a rookie policewoman her last lesson in unarmed combat, huh?"

"Al Wheeler," he said, as a statement of fact. "What's wrong, you mislaid a blonde someplace?"

"If you find her, you can keep her, Bill," I said generously. "I've got a nice little setup here, all ready for your guiding hand."

"O.K.—give!"

"Just one string attached."

"I never got a straight deal out of you yet," he said in a resigned voice.

"The owner is a guy named Ray Willis—book him by all means but make sure he gets bail. I want him loose to commit even greater crimes."

"Whatever you say," Johnson agreed. "Now give me some detail, huh?"

I gave him the name and address of the club, the kind of place it really was.

"Private key club?" he said. "How long you had a key, Al?"

"Long enough," I said smugly. "One of the members is called Denby—known as old man Denby—he got a black eye from one of the girls a couple of nights back—so if you find him he should make a good witness."

"I'll find him," Johnson said confidently. "Inside the next hour that club's coming up with a real double zero."

"I'll tune in for the next installment," I assured him. "See you around, Bill."

"Yeah," he said. "And thanks."

On my way out I stopped to collect my hat from Jerrie Cushman.

"Leaving so soon, Lieutenant?" she said, pouting prettily.

"It's a new trend," I said. "You have a coat? Put it on and go home."

"I'll get fired if I leave this early!" she said.

"You'll get fired anyway, honey," I said tiredly. "It's like that new trend I was telling you about. Everybody gets to be fired, but they get to hear about it downtown and then they got to get their fare home from a bail-bondsman."

"I read you loud and clear, Lieutenant!" she said

quickly. "I get my coat and I'm gone like I was never here."

"It makes me sad—all those lovely sequins going to waste," I said. "But that's show-biz, huh, kid?"

"Right now I see it's no-biz," she said. "Thanks for the tip-off, Lieutenant. If I have trouble getting another job, I'll call you."

"Who cares about jobs?" I said. "Just call me. I have a hi-fi machine in my apartment with five speakers. I can make at least five different drinks without a recipe book. I am a most unusual and interesting character. I can show you life like you never lived it before."

"What else you got in your apartment?" she asked, poker-faced. "A trapeze?"

I drove straight home from the Double Zero, and got into the apartment around ten-thirty. The trouble with being married is that most times you want to be alone you got company waiting for you at home—and the trouble with being a bachelor is most times you want company you get to be alone. I stepped into the apartment and got the best of both worlds. Ilona Brent was sitting in an armchair, waiting for me.

She wore one of those businesslike suits again, with a white, heavy silk blouse underneath. The pixie face looked real cool—maybe cold even.

"How did you get in here?" I asked her.

"I told the janitor if I couldn't get some of my back alimony from you tonight, I'd be thrown out of my apartment," she said calmly. "So he let me in to wait for you."

"I bet that story built my credit rating," I said bleakly.

"He was very nice," Ilona said smiling sweetly. "He said what else could you expect from a lousy, flatfooted cop, and the next time your hi-fi outfit woke him up in the middle of the night, he'd just cut off the power to your apartment until the next morning."

"There's no gratitude," I said morosely. "Nobody has loyalties any more. Only last Christmas I gave him a quarter and this is what I get in return!"

"From the way he was talking, you may get fifty cents' worth yet!"

"Well," I brightened up fast. "This is wonderful—just the girl I wanted to see—I'll go make us a drink and we can talk—or something."

"I don't want a drink," she snapped. "Just the girl you wanted to see, huh? You spent about seven hours in the hotel today but you didn't get around to knocking on my door. Most of the time you were only a wall away, too!"

"Honey," I said in a long-suffering voice, "you know how it is—I'm a cop. Work all the hours around the clock—go where we have to with no choice!"

"You mean it was Lyn's decision you go to bed with her?" she almost snarled.

"With that kind of hearing you must be able to hear the termites as they chew their way through the building," I said in an awed voice.

"Are you implying I sat with my ear to the wall?" she gasped in fury.

"I just dropped in for a drink," I said feebly. "What I can't figure out yet is, how come we're having a fight like we've been married for years when you only came in to see if you could gouge some of the back alimony out of me—and we didn't even get married yet?"

For a long second she fought to keep a straight face, then she dissolved into a helpless wail of laughter. I sneaked out into the kitchen and made a couple of drinks. She'd quieted down to a convulsive giggle that erupted on a five-second frequency by the time I got back.

She took the glass out of my hand, nodding her thanks.

"Lyn told me about it—a confession of triumph," she said when she'd gotten her voice back. "I had to listen and smile, while all the time I wanted to tear out her liver —and it was all your fault!"

"Mine?"

"You should have had some will power and said no. Once she realized you meant it, she wouldn't have bothered you any more."

"I bet you tell that to all the girls," I said gloomily. "But the song of love was kicked off her hit parade tonight. I got it all in words of one syllable to make sure I'd dig the message. That dame is sure different. She doesn't get a seven-year itch like ordinary people—she gets a two-year blight! Hits like lightning, quicker than taxes, and when it does she grabs a man—any man—the nearest man. This year it was Wheeler!"

"The funny thing is, I'm inclined to believe her," Ilona said, sipping her drink idly. "That makes me feel better—not much—just a little."

"I'm happy for you, honey," I said. "Did my faithful sergeant get around to see you before you left the hotel?"

"I knew there was something else I was mad about!" Ilona yelped. "That man is out of his mind—a schizophrenic! I was wearing a negligee when I opened the door, and I guess that was my first mistake. He just stood there—looking. He'd be there now if I hadn't lifted his chin so he *had* to look at my face. Then, when I sat down to answer his questions, he suddenly dived off his chair, skidded across the carpet, and grabbed hold of my foot!"

"He was kicked by a chorus girl when he was very young," I explained. "You dig?"

"It wasn't my foot he wanted!" she said indignantly. "It was my shoe—he wrenched it off, then kept on walking around the room asking me where was the champagne the whole time!"

"Down at the Sheriff's office we call him 'unorthodox,' " I said smugly. "Throws a suspect off-balance all the time."

Ilona's face sobered down suddenly. "How about Hillary?" she asked softly.

"He saw he didn't have a chance so he walked out the window," I said. "Next case, please."

"You don't believe that!" she said tensely.

"The County Sheriff does," I said. "With great reluctance he gave me twenty-four hours to prove him wrong."

"Hillary wasn't exactly my ideal pin-up—"

"Not since you turned seventeen, anyway?"

This got only a puzzled look out of her, so I had to tell her about Hillary's passion for teen-agers. "You never knew it?" I said.

"I never would have even guessed it." She sighed. "Well, he was still a very nice man in many ways."

"How many ways?" I murmured thoughtfully. "I wonder if any of them kept count."

Ilona glared at me. "If you're going to be frivolous all the time I might just as well shut up and not waste my time talking."

"It's only a difference of opinion, honey," I said placatingly. "I don't figure Hillary Summers could have qualified as a nice guy any way you looked at him. He was a weakling with a rare and nasty weakness—not that it entitled him to be pushed out an eighth-story window as the fall guy for the real killer."

"You really don't believe he did it, either!" she said happily. "So what are we arguing about?"

"Tell me something, legal eagle?" I said seriously. "Angela doesn't get any money in her own right until she's twenty-one. Could she make an agreement to give part of her inheritance to someone else when she comes of age?"

"Of course she could," Ilona said, "only she couldn't do it quite so directly as that. It's done all the time—people borrow against money they know is coming to them in the future. All she'd have to do would be make a proper contract with the party concerned, stating that she'd pay the amount within a reasonable time after she reached the age of twenty-one—say six months."

"Would a contract like that have to be notarized?"

"If it was a large sum. You think Angela's borrowed against her inheritance already?"

"No," I said. "I think she could've been blackmailed into signing away a hefty chunk of it. I'd like to know."

"Where would the contract have been signed? Do you have any idea?"

"Right here in Pine City, two days back," I said.

"I'll go to work on it first thing in the morning, if you like," she said enthusiastically. "It shouldn't be too hard to find the notary public who prepared the contract and witnessed the signatures."

"That would be wonderful," I told her. "Now let's relax and play legal fun-games or something. You be a cast-iron contract and I'll be a get-out clause trying to sneak into the contract—torts and caveats can be played wild and—Hey! Where are you going?"

101

"Back to the hotel, lover-man!" she said crisply. "The two-year-blight may be gone, but the memory lingers a little too close right now. Good night, Al." She opened the front door and stepped out into the night.

"I'll give you three caveats to my one tort?" I yelled hopefully, but the door was already closing behind her.

I guessed the guy who first said you can't win all the time was right—the slob!

· 12 ·

POLNIK SAT BESIDE ME IN THE HEALEY, NUDGING ME with his elbow occasionally to make sure I was real. He hadn't recovered from seeing me in the office at nine in the morning yet—maybe he never would. I wondered idly if it would make any difference.

"Where we going, Lieutenant?" he finally managed to ask.

"The motel," I said.

"That crummy joint?" he said in a bewildered voice. "When we could've gone to the Starlight Hotel?—and this early, maybe we'd have caught all the dames in their shirties."

"Shorties!" I gritted my teeth. "It sounds bad enough when you pronounce it right—it's one of those diminutives the world will never forgive Madison Avenue for."

"Is that a fact, Lieutenant?" Polnik said blankly. "I had the Russians figured as the bad guys—with all them spitniks and whoniks and whatever."

"You may well be right," I said hastily.

I parked the car in front of cabin number seven, and climbed out. Polnik eased his bulk out inch by groaning inch, and when he'd finally made it, lumbered across to where I stood in front of the cabin.

"You figuring on buying it, or something, Lieutenant?"

"I was mourning the loss of a photographic genius, Marvin by name," I said. "How many windows does this cabin have, Polnik?"

"Just the one—you're looking through it right now," he added carefully.

"That's one hundred per cent correct. Take a look through the window and tell what you see, Watson."

"Watson?" Polnik tugged at his ear lobe nervously. "I'm Polnik, Lieutenant—you remember me?"

"I was thinking of that sergeant who used to work the narcotics detail one time," I apologized. "Look through the window!"

Polnik did as he was told, his forehead corrugated anxiously. He was a guy who never doubted that a job should be done right—only that he was capable of doing it at all.

"So what do you see?" I asked.

"The inside of the cabin, Lieutenant?"

"Fine—what else?"

"The bed, the bureau—that's about all there is in this crummy passion pit!"

"Where's the bed?" I encouraged him.

"Against the far wall, facing me like."

"Just suppose I was in the cabin right now—lying on the bed. What would I be doing?"

"Looking right at me!" he said triumphantly.

I lit a cigarette and let the smoke combat the strange, early morning air that was a newcomer to my lungs.

"So that's why we mourn the late Albie Marvin," I said. "He was a photographic genius. He got eight pictures of the two of them in the most intimate situations without being noticed—when all either one of them had to do was lift their head a fraction to see him, and his camera, peeking at them through the window."

"You sure he used this window?" Polnik asked.

"It's the only one in the cabin."

"Yeah." He thought about it for a moment. "Maybe he waited until it was dark so they couldn't see him?"

"And used a flash gun?"

103

I heard the heavy footsteps crunching behind me and turned around to greet Mr. Jones.

"You must like this place, Lieutenant?" he said sourly. "You keep on coming back!" He spat contemptuously, adding a fresh stain to the discolored concrete, six inches away from my right shoe.

"Miscalculation," he grunted insolently. "Sorry!"

"You know what I like about beating up an old man, Sergeant?" I said conversationally. "There's no chance of him hitting back."

"They break easy with them brittle bones," Polnik brooded. "But I guess that's because they're old, huh?"

"If you got any business here, state it, Lieutenant!" Jones said harshly. "Or else get off my property!"

"Number seven," I pointed at the cabin in front of us. "The one the young couple stayed in, right?"

"You know it!"

"Number nine." I pointed up the line. "That was Marvin's—right?"

"Some kind of game?" he asked stiffly.

"Right in the middle—number eight," I said. "Open it up for us, Mr. Jones, will you?"

"What for?"

"Because I asked you real polite!"

"You got no right—where's your warrant?" he blustered.

"O.K.," I sighed gently. "Sergeant, there's a health department ordinance that makes spitting an offense within a ten-yard radius of any building that is leased or rented to the general public. Put a pair of bracelets on Mr. Jones and sit him in the car—we'll take him back with us when we go, and book him when we get back into town. Meanwhile, you go and get the keys."

"Yes, sir, Lieutenant!" Polnik beamed.

"All right!" Jones grunted. "I'll get the keys."

I waited while Jones walked stiffly across to his office, with Polnik breathing heavily down his neck. They were back inside two minutes and Jones offered me the key.

"I'd prefer you to open up the cabin," I told him.

He grunted, then turned the key in the lock and pushed the door open. "After you," I said. Inside there was a bed with a bare mattress on top, a bureau to match the ones in the other cabins, and that was about all.

I eased Jones into the bathroom and followed him in. It looked like a beatnik dream of home—there was junk everywhere. Developing tanks, trays of hypo-fixing solution, trays that had dried with a hard brown acid crust. There was a built-in wooden bench along one wall which supported an enlarger. Beside it, stood an expensive-looking 35mm camera with an f/1.8 lens.

"Hobby, Mr. Jones?" I asked politely.

"Any law against it?" He spat into the acid-stained washbowl. "I told you I had a camera!"

"So you did," I agreed.

Back in the other room I took a close look at the dividing wall between the two cabins. You didn't see it till you got real close—the square piece of wood that slid back easily in a greased groove, exposing a circular hole, the exact circumference of the camera lens, I guessed. Whoever used the camera would know the exact distance between the lens and the center of the bed, so the focusing would be automatic. The square of wood could be slid back a fraction of an inch at a time, so the cameraman could peep in on the occupants of the next cabin, until he was sure they were too engrossed to notice the small hole in the wall. Then the camera lens would replace the human eye at the peephole, ready to maybe turn a passing fancy into a permanent record.

"Which do you like best, Mr. Jones?" I asked him. "The peeping, or taking the pictures?"

"Call the Sheriff and ask him to come right out," I told Polnik. "I want him to see this."

The motel proprietor leaned against the wall, his face suddenly ten years older—I wouldn't have believed he could do it and still stay alive.

Lavers came bustling into the cabin a half-hour later, and I showed him the setup with the hole in the wall and the rest of it.

"How did you figure it out?" he asked suspiciously

"Like I said, Sheriff, it was obviously impossible for Marvin to have taken those pictures through the window

—the other possibility that Rickie and Angela posed for the shots didn't seem likely. So it had to be this kind of rigged deal—and that meant Jones had to be in it.

"There were a couple of other pointers—the pictures turned up, but we never found any camera belonging to Marvin. When I checked his billfold there was a hundred bucks in it, but Mrs. Summers had wired him two thousand the morning of the day he was murdered. The murderer could have lifted it out of the billfold—but in that case why leave the hundred? It sounded more like he needed the money for a payoff. Who else could he be paying off in this place but the owner?"

Lavers wrinkled his nose disgustedly. "I don't like this case one little bit. You start figuring you're dealing with a bunch of ordinary people—except one of them's a murderer. Then you get closer to them and you touch nothing but dirt! A piano-player who runs a bordello—a millionaire who buys the favors of high school girls—a woman who wants nothing more than to prove her daughter was raped in the legal sense of the word—and now we got an old man who spends the last days of his life peeping on unsuspecting couples who believed if he didn't give them much else for their money, at least he gave them privacy!"

"Maybe it wasn't a nice thing to do," Jones quavered. "But it ain't no crime!"

"Let's go back to your office, Mr. Jones," I said. "We haven't even started with you yet!"

He sat down heavily in his chair behind the desk as soon as we got inside his office, and stared at the desktop fixedly.

"You ain't got nothing on me!" he said sourly. "And I ain't saying nothing!"

"The photos inside that envelope in Marvin's bag," I said. "Who took them?"

"Marvin, of course!" He glowered at me. "Any fool could tell that—it was his writing on the envelope!"

"How did he take them?"

"I don't know."

"The only way possible was by using that setup of yours," I said. "He couldn't have gotten in there, never mind even known of it, unless you helped him. How much did he pay, Jones?"

"I don't know what you're talking about!"

The Sheriff leaned his hands on the desk, thrusting his neck forward until his face was only a few inches away from the old man's face.

"Listen good, Jones," he said in a low-pitched growl. "You cooperate and I can make it a little easier for you maybe—but if you don't cooperate, I promise you right now you'll die of old age in jail!"

The old man's head twitched suddenly as he stared blindly into Lavers' unblinking eyes.

"All right," he whispered. "What do you want to know?"

"Rickie Willis and Angela Summers arrived," I said. "Then Marvin followed them in by cab an hour later. Take it from there."

"Well, he checked in," Jones mumbled, "and then he asked me some questions—he knew the kids were here all right. He told me he was a private detective and he'd like my help—put fifty bucks on the desktop right in front of me.

"I told him sure I'd help, if I could. Then he tells me the girl is loaded and the kid's a bum who ran off with her. Now he's got them tabbed, he wanted some concrete kind of evidence that they'd been living together, and the only thing he could figure out was to get hold of a camera and bust in on them during the night."

"So you asked him what it would be worth to get a whole series of photos?" I said.

"You're a damned smart aleck!" he said spitefully. "Yeah—and he said a thousand." Jones laughed contemptuously. "What a sucker—overplaying his hand that way. I showed him the setup first and he was hot for it, so then I told him I wanted two thousand or no deal. He cussed me for a while, then he cooled off and said it was a deal. He gave me three hundred on account and said he'd call his client in New York in the morning and get her to wire him some money so he could pay me the rest."

"What was her name?"

"Summers—Mrs. Geoffrey Summers."

"Go on."

"We got the pictures early the next morning, around six, six-thirty." He chuckled evilly. "Hot morning sun always makes the young bucks restless—"

"You can skip the detail," I told him.

"I developed the negatives right after we'd finished, and Marvin was tickled to death when he saw them—he told me to make an extra set of prints. Then he went off to call New York for the dough.

"Later on I saw him talking hard to the boy, and right after that the kid took off in his automobile and didn't get back till around midnight, maybe even later, I'm not sure."

"What else?"

"Came evening and the extra set of prints was ready. I had them in an envelope for him, and he come in here to pick them up. He looked like the cat that's just swallowed the canary—said I did a great job."

"Did he say anything else?" Lavers barked.

"Sure," Jones nodded slowly. "Guess he felt so pleased at himself, he was so goddamned smart, that he just had to tell someone—and there was only me around to tell. Said he was going to clean up a fortune with those pictures—three ways at least."

"How did he figure that out?"

"The kid's mother hired him to find them in the first place—but she hired him through her brother-in-law who was sweet on the kid himself." Jones allowed himself the luxury of one, wheezing guffaw, but the look on Lavers's face shut him up again fast.

"So the kid's uncle tells him to put pressure on her to ditch the young bum—come back to New York and be nice to him again. 'So,' Marvin says, 'I showed the young bum the pictures this morning—threatened him I'd turn them over to the sheriff's office and tell them he was an ex-con at the same time. They'll have him on a rape rap, and maybe the FBI will hit him with a violation of the Mann Act.'

"I can see him now," Jones said reflectively. "Sitting just across the desk from me—right where you are now,

Sheriff—laughing his fool head off. He figured he'd scared the hell out of the boy all ways—told him to take off right then and never come near the girl again or he'd spend the rest of his life in the pen.

" 'So that got rid of the kid,' Marvin said, 'and the mother would be so pleased she'd pay big money.' And a few years from now, when the girl was all set to marry some society character, Marvin figured that would be the time to sell her mother a set of those prints at a very fancy price!"

"Big-mouth Marvin!" I said. "I wonder he lived so long?"

"He was only warming up!" the old man sneered, almost proudy. "I never met a guy with so many angles before —it was like an education."

"You get a close look inside the back of his head?" Lavers asked in a harsh voice. "That was an education, too."

Jones shrugged indifferently. "Next on his list was the girl—he was hot for her. He figured with the Willis kid gone for good, he was going to move in with her that night. He'd show her the pictures, tell her the boy friend had gone forever, and Uncle wanted her back in New York where he could visit with her on a regular basis again. She had no choice—she goes back to her family the next morning—but for the last night at the motel, she'd better be real nice to Marvin or the cops will get the pictures along with the information that Willis is an ex-con."

"Murder in degrees, we got already, Sheriff," I said. "How about a bronze star, or something, for people who murder guys like Marvin?"

"Let's hear the rest and get it finished with, Jones!" Lavers said. "My flesh is starting to crawl."

" 'We got to take care of good old Uncle next'—that's what he said," Jones went on in his slow, grating voice. " 'Watch this!' Marvin told me, then he lifted the phone and called a hotel in Pine City and asked for Hillary Summers. He told Summers he had the pictures, then described them in detail, but along with the pictures, he'd gotten himself a problem.

"The girl's mother wants the photos to use as evidence against the Willis boy, have him indicted for statutory rape. And after the boy's convicted, the mother is sure as hell gonna send the girl off into solitary somewhere—some rest home or something where she'll be out of circulation for a good long time—and Uncle wouldn't like that maybe?"

"The way you tell it, you old goat, we'll be here next week!" Lavers exploded. "So Marvin told Summers he'd sell the pictures to the highest bidder—right?"

"If you know already," the old man said in a surly voice, "why bother asking me?"

"How much did Summers bid?" I asked quickly.

"A hundred grand!" Jones said reverently. "That's what Marvin told me."

"How was it to be paid?"

"Certified bank check—he told Summers they could work out the details later the same night."

"What did you say?" Lavers asked almost politely.

"He told Summers to be here in the motel at eleven," Jones grunted. "Why don't you listen?"

"Did they meet at eleven?" I asked him.

"I wouldn't know," he said listlessly. "I got me a bottle of good liquor and got settled in one of the unrented cabins around nine-thirty—that's the last I remember until sunup next morning."

"Then how did you know Rickie Willis didn't get back until midnight?" I said irritably.

"One of the guests made a complaint in the morning, about him revving his motor in the middle of the night," Jones said triumphantly.

"We've heard enough," Lavers said. "Get him out to my car, Polnik. Don't let any more of him than you can help, touch the upholstery!"

"Sure, Sheriff," Polnik grunted. He heaved the old man onto his feet and guided him out of the office.

"The air's a little cleaner, anyway," Lavers said, after the door closed behind them.

"Mr. Jones," I grinned at him. "One of the Jones boys!"

"Well, Wheeler?" There was a condescending note in

the Sheriff's voice. "I guess that does it up real good!"

"Because that old peeper told us Marvin arranged a meeting with Summers?" I sneered. "What proof you got that Hillary even showed up?"

· 13 ·

ILONA BRENT SMILED A WELCOME AT ME AS I WALKED into her hotel suite. I ran the smile through my little gray computors and got only a "platonic-plus" reading.

"It's lunchtime," I said. "So I figured you might buy me lunch."

She wore a white orlon sweater, over a pair of tight, gray cotton slacks, and somehow it gave her that healthy, outdoor-sexy look you read about in English novels, where the heroine's always called Pamela.

"Lunch is a good idea, Al," Ilona said. "Why don't we eat here? I'll have room service bring it up. What do you feel like right now?"

"Are we still talking about food?"

"But definitely!"

"A thick, rare, and bloody steak," I said. "With a French salad on the side."

"Is that all?"

"For me, it's a big deal," I assured her.

She called room service, then made us a drink, still radiating an air of "Miss Efficiency, 1960," which was irritating to a disorganization man like myself. Then she sprang her big story, and I could dig the efficiency bit.

"I found him, Al," she said with elaborate casualness.

"How long was he lost?" I asked absently.

"Don't be a moron! The notary public—I found him!"

"Oh—him!" I was suddenly a lot more interested.

"You were right," she said quickly. "Seventy-five thousand dollars to Ray Willis, for services rendered, to be paid not later than six months after she reaches twenty-one."

"You sure worked fast, Ilona!" I congratulated her.

"I'm a pretty damned smart attorney," she said complacently.

"Or you will be—when you get out from under the Summers family," I said.

Her face flushed violently. "That's a stinking thing to say!"

"Why? Because it's true?"

The food arrived, saving her the trouble of finding an answer. We ate—and when we were finished, I gave her a quick run-down on the motel's special facilities for peeping and candid camera work, then old man Jones' story of Marvin's conniving blackmail schemes.

"It's fantastic, Al!" Ilona said breathlessly. "You wouldn't believe one man could be so—evil!"

"There was plenty of it around he could draw on," I said soberly. "Do you still want to help?"

"Of course I do," she said determinedly. "I told you last night I knew Hillary never killed Marvin."

"You could end up wishing he had!" I warned her.

"I'll take my chances on that," she said defiantly.

"O.K.," I grinned bleakly, "so now we're in business."

She leaned her elbow on the table, her chin cupped in her hand, staring at me earnestly; and I wondered uneasily if she was about twenty years too young for the caper I had in mind.

"Shoot!" she said suddenly. "Lay out the plan of campaign, General!"

"Let's start with Hillary. If he didn't commit suicide, he must have been murdered because he knew who killed Marvin—and the killer was scared Hillary might crack under pressure and talk."

"I'm still with you," Ilona nodded gravely.

"Right now, the killer is feeling safe and secure—the Sheriff's office thinks Hillary's death was suicide and blame him for the murder. That makes it too late for questions, clues, and all that kind of jazz. The only way we can get him now is to put a bomb under his tail, and hope he'll jump before he has time to think."

"A brilliant thesis, General!" She gave me an exaggerated salute.

"Keep listening," I said drily. "You could change your mind fast. At the same time we plant the bomb, we've got to make it look like it can be deloused without much trouble or risk on his part. You dig?"

I was suddenly dazzled by the warm, shining glow in her eyes.

"I truly admire you, Al!" she said in a hushed voice. "It must take an awful lot of cold courage to set yourself up as a clay pigeon."

"Not me, honey." I shook my head sadly. "You!"

"Me!"

"Sorry," I apologized, "but the casting is perfect—nobody else can play the bit."

"My hero!" she said bitterly. "Here I am, thinking all kinds of noble thoughts about you, while all the time you're setting me up as a—" Her spine straightened with a sudden jerk. "Hey! They shoot clay pigeons!"

"You can gracefully decline," I said mildly. "Nobody's going to think badly of you—like they used to tell the paratroops the moment before they booted them out of the plane."

"Maybe I'll think about it," she said cautiously. "Tell me exactly what your sneaking, cowardly mind has cooked up."

"Your story goes something like this," I said. "Yesterday morning Hillary came to you, as the family's attorney, gave you a sealed envelope, and said to do nothing with it unless he suddenly died during the next seven days. If that happened, you were to open the envelope."

"It sounds grisly," Ilona shivered.

"You opened the envelope this morning. Inside was another sealed envelope and a list of instructions. First, you had to call the four people listed, and tell them in accordance with his wishes that the second envelope would be opened exactly twenty-four hours after his death and the contents read aloud to them at the Travelers' Rest Motel."

"Now I know you're crazy!" she said.

"Who's going to shoot at a clay pigeon sitting on the County Sheriff's desk? It has to be someplace where the killer figures he's got more than a sporting chance."

"I'm ahead of you, Al!" she said brightly. "I'm supposed to open the envelope at eight-ten tonight, but a couple of hours before, you'll have a truckload of Sheriff's men well-hidden all around the—"

"You blew the bit again," I said sorrowfully, "not a chance! The killer would smell it a mile away. There's going to be just you and the four others—and me. No one but you will know I'm there, I hope."

"You make it sound irresistible," Ilona said dully, "like typhoid!"

"At least one of them is going to ask why you didn't give the sealed envelope to the police right away," I warned her. "You say Hillary's instructions called for the strictest secrecy, and as his attorney, you'll see his wishes carried out."

Ilona nodded dismally. "When do we start?"

"Right now," I said. "Call them before they make other plans for the evening."

"Who are they?"

"Lyn and Angela Summers, Rickie and Ray Willis."

"And one of them is a murderer?" she asked nervously.

"I don't have any other suspects—outside you and me," I said reasonably.

"Where would I find Ray Willis?"

"I'm not sure—his club's out of operation now. Ask Rickie, he'll know."

"What do we do after that—until eight o'clock tonight?"

"Make the calls first," I suggested. "We can worry about that later. Remember, you must make it sound real good! If anyone even thinks it could be a gag, we'll have blown the bit. Then we can sit around here the rest of the afternoon with egg all over our faces."

"I'll make it good!" she said determinedly.

"That's my girl," I said. "Probably all of them will want to see the envelopes and instruction list, so you'll have to brush them off fast and hard—don't give them a chance to bounce back."

"I'll say I couldn't possibly give any one of them an unfair advantage over the other three?" Ilona suggested.

"Fine! Go to it."

She called Mrs. Geoffrey Summers first, and hung up on her three minutes later while Lyn was still asking questions. Angela was next, then Rickie, who told her she could contact his brother at the Central Hotel, in the heart of downtown Pine City. It was another fleabag along with the Grand, I remembered.

Ilona was an expert by the time Ray Willis answered the phone. She gave him the facts neatly leaving nothing out, then replaced the receiver before he'd even got around to framing the first question.

"That was great!" I told her. "You did fine."

"I'm glad it's over, anyway." She flopped onto the couch. "I'm positive they all took it seriously. What do we do now?"

"Why don't I make us a drink?"

"Fine," she said. "What then?"

"We'll just sit around and drink some more," I said. "If we're right, and one of those four people is the real murderer, he, or she, thinks you've got a sealed letter exposing him—so figure it out for yourself."

"I'm not too sure I want to," she said cautiously. "You spell it out for me?"

I made the drinks and walked them back toward the couch. "He knows at a little after eight tonight you'll be at the motel, ready to open the envelope. So he's got from now until then to make sure it doesn't get opened."

Ilona closed her eyes and shivered violently. "You mean he's going to come here looking for it! Stay close to me, Al!"

Then she gave a sudden shriek and opened her eyes wide.

"Is that close enough?" I asked innocently.

Around four-thirty, there was a sudden, loud knocking on the door which made Ilona leap convulsively.

"Take it easy," I whispered. "I'll be in the bedroom—play it cool, and if it looks like it's getting rough, I'll be in."

"Don't hesitate, Al!" she said fervently. "If somebody bats an eyelash even, I want you to come running."

I catfooted into the bedroom, nearly closing the door, leaving a thin crack through which I could see most of the living room. Ilona opened the door, and I heard Rickie Willis' gruff voice.

They came into my line of vision as Ilona brought him across to the couch, then sat down.

"Won't you sit down?" she said politely.

Rickie scratched the top of his crewcut and gave her a hostile stare. "I didn't come here to play no games, sister," he said thickly. "I want that envelope you got."

"Envelope?" Ilona repeated weakly.

"Don't play it dumb," he rasped. "You called Angie and me and told us all about it a couple hours back. I want it!"

"What for?"

"I got my reasons!"

Ilona shook her head dubiously. "I can't give it to you, Rickie. Hillary Summers made some specific instructions as to how it should be handled, and I have to do it that way because I'm his attorney. I'm sure you understand."

"Hillary Summers!" he snarled. "The nut! He was crazy—you must have known that! He could've put anything in that letter—any crazy thing at all!"

"Well"— Ilona's voice had a false note of brightness— "we'll all know at ten after eight tonight, won't we?"

"No!" He leaned down until his savage, brooding face was only a few inches away from hers. "Because you're going to give it to me now, and I'm burning it!"

"Why?"

"I told you—don't tell me you've lost your marbles, too!" he said disgustedly. "That nut, Hillary, could've written anything at all. Like it wasn't him that knocked off the septic eye—like it was somebody else maybe."

"Why would he say you did it, if you didn't?" Ilona's voice shook slightly.

"Me?"

He straightened up again, a look of blank amazement on his face. "Man! Somebody send for the little men in the big white coats!" His head shook slowly. "You need help, lady! Why in hell would I knock off the septic eye? He didn't worry me."

"Then why do you want Hillary's letter if you're sure it doesn't accuse you of the murder?" Ilona asked.

Rickie dug a crumpled pack of cigarettes out of his leather jacket, stuck one into his mouth, and lit it, dragging the smoke down into his lungs impatiently.

"I don't wanna get tough with you, lady," he said thickly, "not unless I got to. So maybe I'll give it to you slow—just one more time. I want that letter because Hillary was out of his mind—he was crazy for Angie all the time—and when Angie took off with me, he flipped! Now, you dig? So before he makes like an elevator out an eight-floor window, he writes a letter and gives it to you, huh? What better way's he got to get his revenge against Angie? Say it was her killed the septic eye, not him! A dead man always bugs people—they'll believe it!"

"I see," Ilona said faintly.

"That's where you're wrong again, sister!" he snarled. "Not you, not anybody else either, gets to see that letter, because I'm putting a match to it right now!"

There was a second knock on the door, and Rickie moved his shoulders uneasily under the leather jacket.

"Go find out who that is," he said. "Tell 'em to go away!"

Ilona got up from the couch and went to the door. A moment later she backed away from it as Ray Willis followed her into the room, a gun in his hand.

Behind him came Angela, wearing the black, stretch-nylon pants with the vivid yellow sweater again. The bird's-nest hair-do was a little more groomed than usual, and her big, dark eyes held a look of excited anticipation.

Rickie's mouth dropped open as he saw the two of them. "What goes on?" he asked sullenly. "Who asked you to the party? I can handle this on my own!"

"I got to your room just after you left," Ray snapped. "She told me where you'd gone. Why didn't you stay out of it, you dumb ox?"

"Lay off, Ray!" Rickie scowled at his brother, his shoulders moving again under the jacket. "You're not so smart—letting that dumb lieutenant close you up!"

Angela sauntered past Ray toward Rickie, moving with a feline, animal grace that went a long way toward explaining, if not excusing, Hillary Summers. She put her elbow on Rickie's shoulder, leaning her body against him provocatively as she looked at Ilona.

"Did she give you the letter yet, honey?" she asked in a childish drawl.

Rickie's mouth turned down at the corners. "Not yet."

"See?" Ray sneered. "I told you, kid, you don't have the know-how to handle a thing like this right."

"Ah, why don't you go——"

"Don't get mad at Ray, lover-man," Angela giggled excitedly. "Let's get the letter from her."

"That's what I've been trying to do!" Rickie took a deep breath. "What a dame! Yack, yack, yack! I think I'm blowing my stack listening to her questions! I'm trying to keep it polite because I don't want to get rough and——"

"Tell us some other time," Ray said curtly. "Let's get what we came for and get out of here."

Angela held out her hand to Ilona. "The letter please, Counselor."

"I can't give it to you," Ilona said doggedly. "I've got to obey Hillary's instructions, and——"

"Did he instruct you, too?" Angela giggled again. "He had a lot of cute tricks, didn't he?"

"Shut up!" Rickie growled.

"I didn't know he went for older women." Angela's voice had a shrill sound to it. "Did you enjoy the preliminary routine, Miss Brent? I always figured it was monotonous, but Hillary used to get a big bang out of it. You know, first, he'd make you take——"

She stopped suddenly as Rickie's fist drove into her ribs with brutal precision. The pain sharpened her face into hard, drawn lines so she looked twenty years older.

"I said for you to shut up!" Rickie slurred the words

118

thickly, meshing them together in an indistinct growl. "All the time you keep talking about that slob—all the time! Why do you keep on, huh? The bum is dead all right, isn't he? It was you lined him up, all hot and eager, in front of that window and then gave him a shove, wasn't it?"

He stopped suddenly, gaping at her, his eyes almost pleading.

"You stupid moron!" Ray said bitterly. "You know what you've done?"

"Yeah," Rickie shrugged petulantly. "It's her fault, the teasing bitch! She gets me so mad all the time I dunno what I'm saying."

"Now we've got to do something about her," Ray said sharply, nodding toward Ilona.

Angela took a deep, shuddering breath, still massaging her ribs with her left hand. "What, Ray?" The excited anticipation bubbled in her voice. "What are you going to do? Can I help, please, Ray, please?"

He shook his head wearily. "Sometimes I wonder how I ever got mixed up with you two weirdos—I must have been out of my mind!"

"Yeah—seventy-five grand's worth!" Rickie sneered.

Ray walked slowly toward Ilona, who shrank back as he got close. He moved his arm up even more slowly, until the barrel of his gun was touching her forehead.

"We don't have any more time to kid around, lady," he said in a deceptively mild voice. "The letter?"

She swallowed twice before she could speak, "It's—it's in the bedroom."

"Then we'll go get it," he said.

"It's all right," she said frantically. "I know where it is, I'll get it! There's no need for you to come too."

"Uh-uh," he said, shaking his head. "You might be thinking of doing something cute—like throwing it out the window, maybe?"

"Of course not!" Ilona quavered. "I just thought—"

"Bad habit!" Ray shook his head reprovingly. "Buy yourself a load of grief that way. Let's go get it now, huh?"

"It's in the second drawer of the bureau—under an evening purse!" she said desperately.

"Now you're being smart," Ray said with a grin. "Get it, Rickie!"

I moved back against the wall, so when Rickie opened the door it would cover me. His footsteps thumped heavily across the room, getting louder all the time, until the door swung open suddenly.

He moved straight across the room toward the bureau, kicking the door shut behind him with unnecessary force —maybe he imagined it was his brother's face.

I moved out from the wall with the thirty-eight in my hand, and a second later he saw my reflection in the bureau mirror. He stopped abruptly, standing very still, his eyes watching my reflection with the absolute concentration of a cornered animal.

"No noise, Rickie," I said softly. "Turn around."

He turned to face me, his arms dangling loosely at his sides. I checked with my free hand and found he wasn't carrying a gun.

"O.K.," I said. "Let's go and join the party. I'm going to be right behind you, Rickie-boy, so if you get any fancy ideas about brother Ray getting in a fast shot, just remember he's got to shoot through you!"

"I hear you—cop!" he said tightly.

He opened the door again and stepped out into the living room, with me right behind him.

"You get it?" Ray turned his head to look, and saw the two of us.

"Drop the gun, Ray!" I said sharply. "You got just two seconds!"

He opened his fingers and the gun dropped to the carpet.

"How did he get in there?" he snarled at Rickie.

"He was already there—he must've been there all the time," Rickie said.

"You mean you never even cased the apartment when you first got inside?" Ray almost screamed. "Why, you stupid, dumb—"

"Don't keep on calling me them names!" Rickie growled. "I get tired, all the time you calling me names!"

Ray closed his eyes in anguish for a couple of seconds, then opened them slowly. "What's the use?" he said

120

limply. "You let him con us all the way down the line."
He looked at me dully. "No letter, huh?"

"No letter, Ray," I agreed.

"Strictly a come-on?"

"Yeah."

Angela cleared her throat gently, then smiled at me.
"Hi, Lieutenant!"

"You lined him up in front of the window then gave
him a shove?" I repeated Rickie's words gently.

Her smile broadened. "It seemed like the best thing
to do at the time. You see, Hillary had a date with
Marvin that night, at the motel, but he was late. Marvin
figured he wasn't going to show up, so he came to the
cabin and showed me those pictures. I was all through,
he told me, he'd scared Rickie so hard I'd never see him
again. And in the morning he was giving me back to dear
old Mom. She'd take me back to New York, where Hillary was going to make sure he kept me in line!"

Her smile started to get a fixed look about it. "Not
much of a future for a girl, was it? But Marvin was only
starting, I found that out quickly. He was going to spend
the rest of the night with me, he said, and if I objected
he'd give the pictures to the police and have Rickie arrested for rape. With his prison record, Rickie wouldn't
stand a chance, he said, he'd go to jail for the rest of
his life!"

"So you killed him?" I said.

She nodded, almost casually. "I couldn't bear him to
touch me—a dirty little man with cruel, filthy eyes. I knew
he was going to hurt me—he'd get his kicks that way.
Then I remembered the old hammer I'd seen in the bottom drawer of the bureau. I told him I wanted to pick
up a couple of things and then I'd go to his cabin with
him—that would be better in case Rickie came back. So
I got this real sexy nylon gown I have and carried the
hammer with it, right into his cabin. I pretended I was
getting excited about the idea of spending the night with
Marvin, and the little monster believed it. I told him to
turn around and not peek for a moment while I took
off my clothes."

She giggled again, helplessly. "He looked so funny,

121

standing there solemnly gazing at the wall, having fantasies about what he was going to do with me—and all the time the hammer was lifting higher . . . higher . . . higher . . ."

The whites of her eyes showed briefly, then she collapsed in a limp heap onto the floor. I stepped toward her, moving in front of Ray Willis deliberately, being careful not to look at him.

Ilona was down on her hands and knees beside Angela, trying to do something for her. My spine did a tango as I heard the sudden, furtive moment behind me. I gave him one more second, then turned around.

Ray was coming up off his knees, with the gun he'd grabbed off the floor in his hand.

"I said I'd get you, Wheeler!" he snarled, as the gun barrel swung toward me in a short arc.

I pulled the trigger of the thirty-eight three times, watching the triumphant grin on his face dissolve suddenly as the slugs hammered through flesh and bone to lodge in his brain. He slid sideways to the floor and was dead by the time he reached it.

Rickie hadn't moved; there was a secretive look in his eyes as he stared down at his brother's body, almost a look of satisfaction.

Ilona was staring at me blankly, her eyes quick-frozen.

"How's Angela?" I asked curtly, hoping it would snap her out of it.

"Angela?" she repeated slowly. Then her eyes came alive again. "She's all right, I think, Al. She must have just passed out with the emotional pressure, or something."

I moved over to the phone, keeping a watchful eye on Rickie while I called the Sheriff's office.

When I'd finished, Ilona got to her feet and looked at me. "I don't know what it is, but she won't come round —her breathing seems normal."

"I told them to bring a doctor," I said. "I could use a drink—how about making us one?"

"Yes, sir!" she breathed heavily. "What about him?" She nodded toward Rickie.

"Why not?" I shrugged.

She started to make the drinks, then looked at me again. "Did you know it was Angela all the time?"

"I wasn't sure until Hillary went out that window," I said. "I guess you couldn't blame Angela too much for using sex to get what she wanted, not after the kind of introduction she'd had. You remember you told me she visited with you that night, then went off to see her mother, but didn't? When she came back, she was waving a wad of notes around—and her face was flushed, with a kind of triumphant look?"

"She went to see Hillary of course," Ilona nodded. "The money came from him and . . . oh, I see."

"Sure you do," I said. "Hillary was the kind of guy who would have been too embarrassed to kill himself unless he looked his best! So it figured that Thursday night when he went out the window was just a carbon copy of Wednesday night when she got the money from him— except with a different ending."

"Lieutenant," Rickie was mumbling, "I didn't have nothing to do with killing the septic eye—that's honest!"

"I'll believe it," I told him. "My guess is Hillary showed up late for his meeting with Marvin—just about the time Angela was leaving Marvin's cabin. Being Hillary, he wouldn't help her, but he didn't want her in jail either. So he did nothing, just kept his mouth shut."

I looked at Rickie again. "When you came back, she told you what had happened?"

"Yeah," he nodded. "She had the pictures and we burned 'em. We didn't know there was more of them— figured they were the only ones he had!"

"Early next morning you went to see big brother, Ray, to get him to help," I said. "He cooked up that stupid Nevada story and faked a marriage certificate for you— at a price. That made me wonder when I heard about it —it wasn't even a serious attempt to alibi you. Angela must have had one hell of a guilty conscience to pay that kind of money for the punk service Ray gave her!"

" 'Get smart!' he said." Rickie looked at his brother's body again. "All the time he'd keep on at me I was a stupe, a moron, a dumb one!" A slow smile crept across his face,

"Me—I'm the dumb one all right—I'm the one that's still alive!"

Angela moaned softly, then slowly sat up, staring at me with her enormous dark eyes a complete blank.

"You feeling better, Angela?" I asked her.

Her lips moved rapidly but no sound came from them.

"Angela!" Ilona said sharply. "Are you all right?"

Slowly the head turned in the direction of Ilona's voice, then she stared at her for maybe ten long seconds without saying anything, while Ilona cringed away from the blank, staring eyes.

"Hey, Angie!" Rickie said uneasily. "Say something, huh, baby? You giving me the creeps, just sitting there, doing nothing. Wassa matter, baby? You sick or something?"

Her lips writhed, then suddenly she spoke, her voice a harsh, discordant croak.

"Mom?" The blank eyes looked around the room slowly. "I want my mom!"

"All passengers for Flight Six-Thirteen, Los Angeles, Chicago, and New York, should proceed to Gate Six immediately!" The metallic voice boomed through the airport lounge.

"That's us," Ilona said in a small voice.

"I shall go now," Lyn Summers said in a precise voice. "Be careful you don't miss the plane, Ilona!"

"I'll be there," Ilona said easily.

Mrs. Geoffrey Summers adjusted the collar of her white chinchilla jacket a little closer around her neck, and moved toward the gate. Her ice-cold eyes looked at me, then through me, for the last time. Then she was gone.

"She could have spoken one word anyway," Ilona said. "The last thirty minutes she's been with us, you didn't even exist!"

"Why do you bother going back to New York with her?" I asked. "You don't owe her a thing."

"Hillary dead—her daughter a murderess," Ilona said softly. "She needs somebody to look after her now!"

"With the kind of money she has, she could buy the

124

Waldorf-Astoria and turn it into a private residence," I said. "Then she'd have so many servants, she could—"

"There's no one now except me she can even talk to, Al," Ilona said. "Draw your own moral—the things that money—"

"And all that jazz!" I finished the tag. "O.K. I'll miss you."

"I'll miss you, Al." She smiled. "It was fun in a kind of unorthodox way!"

"Last call for Flight Six-Thirteen," the loudspeakers blared.

"I must go!" she said. "Did you hear any more about Angela?"

"A catatonic trance, the doc said. When the load gets too great, the mind refuses to carry it any more, then—nothing."

"It's horrible!" she whispered. "What will they do to her?"

"Plead insanity, put her into a sanitarium," I said. "You never can tell about those things—maybe one day she'll be cured."

"I hope so!" She kissed my cheek suddenly. "I have my bruises in everloving memory!" Then she ran toward the gate at a fast clip, just making it on board the plane.

After the plane had left, I went back to the Healey and drove into town. It looked like it was going to be a lonely night. I debated visiting with Sheriff and Mrs. Lavers—then remembered the look on his face when I told him he'd been wrong about Hillary, and decided against the visit. That way, I was still alive, if lonely.

It was about nine-thirty when I parked outside the apartment building and I hadn't been home that early in years. I met the janitor in the lobby, and watched his gray hair bristle when he saw me.

"Cheater!" he mumbled loudly.

I thumbed the elevator button, then looked at him. "What did you say?"

"They got special rules for cheating cops so they don't go to jail like other folks?" he asked belligerently.

"Don't tell me," I said. "You just lost your mind—I'll help you look for it."

"Least you could do is pay the alimony!" he snarled.

The elevator arrived and the door slid open. I stepped forward, still watching him curiously.

"How many wives have you got!" he exploded.

The sliding door wiped him off, leaving me wondering. I was still wondering when I opened the front door of the apartment and walked in. Now it was my turn for the funny farm. The lights were on, the hi-fi machine was oozing music through the five speakers. . . .

"Cigarettes?" a husky voice asked.

A stunning blonde wearing a black sequined bra and tights sauntered out to meet me.

"Jerrie Cushman!" I said slowly.

"You said for me to call you, Lieutenant," she said demurely. "I called and called, but you weren't answering, so I thought I'd come over and wait for you to get home."

"How did you get into the apartment?"

She dimpled. "I hope you don't get mad at me, Lieutenant. I told the janitor I was your ex-wife and if I didn't get to see you tonight—"

"—and pick up some of the back alimony, you'd be thrown out of your own apartment!" I finished for her.

"I thought it was original!" She shrugged her beautiful, honey-tanned shoulders. "He took a lot of convincing. Asked me how many wives you had—so naturally I told him just the one, me. Then he got all sympathetic and kept shaking his head and saying, 'You poor little thing, you don't know. . . .' Is he a screwball?"

"I'm working on it," I said. "But you helped a lot, Jerrie, believe me!"

I followed her into the living room where the lights were subdued, the music soft, and two tall drinks stood waiting on top of a small table in front of the couch.

"I thought I'd make things comfy, Lieutenant," Jerrie murmured.

"Al's the name," I said absently. "Comfy?"

"I need the job," she said in a mocking voice. "Sit down, honey. Cigarette?"

"No, thanks," I said happily as I sat down on the couch.

126

"I have the drinks ready." She sat down, but on my lap instead of the couch. "Is there anything else I can do for you?"

"I know show-biz is a tough racket, Jerrie," I said, patting her thigh sympathetically. "But I'm just an easy-going cop—have your drink first!"

Other SIGNET Suspense Stories
You'll Want to Read